A Very GOOD CHANCE

Also by Sarah Moore Fitzgerald

Back to Blackbrick
The Apple Tart of Hope

A Very GOOD CHANCE

Sarah Moore Fitzgerald

Orion
Children's Books

ORION CHILDREN'S BOOKS

First published in Great Britain in 2016 by
Hodder and Stoughton

1 3 5 7 9 10 8 6 4 2

Text © Sarah Moore Fitzgerald, 2016

The moral rights of the author have been asserted.

A CIP catalogue record for this book
is available from the British Library.

ISBN 978 1 4440 1478 5

Printed and bound by CPI Group (UK) Ltd, Croydon, CR0 4YY

The paper and board used in this book are from
well-managed forests and other responsible sources.

Orion Children's Books
An imprint of
Hachette Children's Group
Part of Hodder and Stoughton
Carmelite House
50 Victoria Embankment
London EC4Y 0DZ

An Hachette UK Company

www.hachette.co.uk

www.hachettechildrens.co.uk

For Elizabeth Moore

1

Ned Buckley and Martin Cassidy joined our class in the middle of the winter term, and to start with, you never saw one of them without the other. They had the same walk and the same silent way and the same brooding expressions on their faces. Otherwise they weren't in the slightest bit alike. Martin's eyes were pale and small. He had a round face and red hair and when he closed his fists, his fingers turned purple.

Ned's hands were tanned and so was his face. His eyes were large and so dark that he could have been wearing mascara. Though knowing Ned Buckley that would be unlikely. I remember how from the very start Laura had kept nudging me to tell me to quit staring. But I couldn't stop looking at him.

Serena Serralunga, our history teacher, said we should make an effort to get to know them, but it's not that easy to get to know people who never speak and who don't look at anyone when they come into class and who disappear at random times of the day for no obvious reason.

Martin Cassidy stayed for eighteen days and then disappeared for good. Soon, I couldn't recall that much about him except for the redness of his hair and the purpleness of his fists. We hadn't made much of an effort, but to be fair, he hadn't given us much of a chance.

Serena Serralunga said that there are times when the only thing a person needs is someone to hold out a friendly hand or show them where the vending machine is or say a single word of kindness – and those small things can convince someone to stay in school when they're thinking of maybe leaving.

I don't remember anyone even trying to talk to Martin or Ned in the early days – because why would we when everyone in my class would much prefer to talk about people behind their backs? That's Ballyross Secondary for you. And Brendan Kirby is our king.

The news went round that Martin Cassidy had had an accident. Serena Serralunga said he'd fallen off a horse, and Brendan Kirby snorted with laughter in this special way he had when he was being entertained by someone else's bad luck.

Maybe he wouldn't have laughed so hard if something like that had happened to Dougie or Laura or even me, but then again maybe he would have. Other people's misfortune is the kind of thing Brendan has always found hilarious – and he had a particular thing about

Martin Cassidy and Ned Buckley.

If I'm honest, everyone had a thing about them. The reasons for that are complicated and difficult to explain.

I remember the first day I ever heard Ned Buckley's voice. Brendan was sitting in the back row, with his usual crew organised in a circle around him.

'He rides with a bunch of wild boys across the river,' he said. 'And he's broken his coccyx. Anyone know what that is?' To Brendan's delight, nobody did. 'It's his tailbone! Ha. And now he and his broken bum are moving. His family never stays anywhere for long, you see.'

Everyone nodded their heads as if Brendan was the birthplace of all knowledge.

Nobody'd noticed that Ned Buckley was sitting at his desk in the far corner. He got up slowly and walked over to where Brendan was sitting.

Ned had been so permanently silent and unreadable for such a long time that if he'd grown wings and flown up above our heads, we couldn't have been more surprised.

'You shouldn't talk about things you don't understand,' was what he said, and he stared at us for a while, and his voice was deliberate and strong, and we just kept looking back at him with our mouths open.

After he'd said that, Ned did what he always did at the end of school, which was to walk out of the door without looking back.

I still think about how his words affected us – how he'd broken his silence, and how the reason he'd done it was to stop Brendan's maliciousness on the subject of Martin Cassidy from spreading – which, to be honest, Brendan's maliciousness on the subject of anything often did.

After that, a few things began to change in our class. They weren't very dramatic, but they were noticeable all the same. For example, from then on, Brendan always looked around the room before sitting down with his group to talk about anyone.

2

There is a tunnel made of trees at the beginning of Nettlebog Lane. It's a twisty narrow road that leads down to the river and there's a scraggly strip of grass growing along the middle of it.

Once you've walked through, you're near the part of the bank where the water's at its widest and it looks like it goes on forever. It feels like being in the middle of a secret – as if you're skirting the edges of something risky and wrong. There's this big curvy bend in the river – it's called the Giant's Elbow and right in the crook of it is a lush circle of trees. Even in the winter, when Nettlebog seems like the craggiest, most windswept place in the world, that particular bunch of trees stays green and dark and thick and tall.

Whenever you're down there, you get a mad, free kind of feeling that makes you want to shout.

Most grown-ups are normally very keen on anything that gets you out in the fresh air, but to the parents of Ballyross, Nettlebog is out of bounds. There are loads of reasons why nobody is supposed to go there.

They say it is on account of the river's strong current and because there are no lights on either side of the water's edge.

Parents seem to think that things will happen to you if you go down to Nettlebog. There's a theory that anyone who does will instantly slip into the water and drown.

It was Laura who told me that someone *had* drowned there, but Laura's a bit of a drama queen, so you can't always be sure about a lot of the stuff she says. If you Google 'drowning, Nettlebog' or 'Nettlebog drowning' or even 'death Nettlebog Lane' or any other combination, there's no mention of it, so I reckon it's one of those urban myths that frightens everyone into staying away.

But if you look at the water more closely and how deep it is and how dark, and how it licks the rocky bank and suddenly swells and rises unexpectedly – then the possibility of drowning doesn't seem too crazy.

You can drown in a puddle. Nettlebog river is much deeper than that.

When I was younger I used to like it when Mum and Dad said, 'Arminta, you are not to go to Nettlebog.'

Those were the days when I did what I was told, and

when I didn't mind being called Arminta. Doing what I was told used to make me feel safe.

But lots of things have changed. First of all, people call me Minty now. And secondly there was a new feeling inside me – a feeling that it's a pain in the neck to have parents who are constantly telling me what to do. And OK, I get it, parents don't like you to gather at a place where somebody has possibly drowned. It goes against their instincts. But I'd begun to realise that parents can't decide everything. There were things I needed to make up my own mind about.

And on top of that there is this thing about Nettlebog that had a way of pulling me towards it. The way music sometimes does, or colour. Plus, there was a tangled magic smell that's like no other: herb and nut and wood and bog. I liked breathing those smells in and I liked the way they filled my head and made me feel confident and calm, but sort of excited too, the way mystifying places do.

I was the one who went to Nettlebog first. Or should I say, I thought I was.

It turns out that practically everyone who goes there thinks they're the first. It turns out I'm not the only one who felt those feelings. Dougie told me he used to think *he* was the only person who knew about it.

'Same,' said Laura when we told her. We made this promise to each other that from then on, we'd never go unless we went together. It was kind of a pact that we had, I'm not sure why.

That was when there were still lots of things about it

we didn't know. For example, we didn't know that hidden behind the thick circle of trees, there was a caravan, and we didn't know that inside that caravan, two people lived, and we didn't know that one of those people was Ned Buckley.

3

It might have taken much longer to find out if it hadn't been for the bonfire and the shed. There were two horses down there too – and they belonged to Ned. And they weren't dangerous or wild like some people said. One was brown and black, the other palest grey. Both of them were perfectly beautiful. Ned built the shed for the horses. We could hear the hammering and banging for days.

The trees seemed thicker and bushier, like somehow they could grow faster than normal trees do. They closed around the caravan like a fortress – right there at the water's edge.

One night, very late, long after I was supposed to be asleep, I could smell something smoky drifting in, and there was the pop and crackle of an outside fire. I slid out of bed, went over to sit by my open window. Strange shapes flickered and flashed in my room.

'NETTLEBOG's ON FIRE!' Dougie had texted.

His little sister had run in and woken him, claiming

there was a dragon dancing in the middle of the water, he said.

I thought about calling the fire services, but even though it was bright and dramatic-looking, Dougie and I agreed that the fire didn't actually look as if it was out of control. In the end we didn't do anything except watch in the dark.

When I finally decided to go to sleep, everything had faded to a pale orange smudge in the blackness.

Dougie and Laura and I went down next day after school. There was a rusted battered white van that I hadn't seen before, and from the massive oak tree that leaned out over the water, someone had hung a rope with a tyre swinging from the end of it.

That was the thing about Nettlebog – it seemed completely different from everywhere else in our lives. Ballyross Grove where we lived was right next to it, but it didn't have tall enough trees or wide enough spaces for something as gigantic as a swing like that.

Ballyross Grove is a cul-de-sac. The houses are on a curve, bunched together. Whichever pavement you stand on, the houses opposite seem like faces squashed up beside each other with rectangular door mouths and square window eyes. Everything neat and safe and tidy and in order.

We were curious then, and interested and drawn to the light of Nettlebog and the noise that had begun to come from there – but even though we didn't say it, I think we were kind of annoyed too. Nettlebog had been our place.

It was *our* secret. And now we realised Ned was there, making it bright in the night and hanging swings off its trees and acting as if it belonged to him.

Dougie leaned out of his window an awful lot after that – looking towards Nettlebog. He saw Ned swinging on the black tyre.

'Flying over and back he was, above the water. And he was roaring.'

'What was he roaring?' I asked.

'Dunno,' Dougie said. 'Something loud.'

Ned Buckley was our next-door neighbour. He lived in the middle of the mystery that was Nettlebog.

I imagined what it would be like to be friends – actual, real, proper friends – with Ned Buckley. The idea settled inside my head like a precious thing.

According to Brendan, though, Ned was not friend material. Apparently everyone was kind of scared of him. Apparently Ned Buckley was no good.

4

Ned was the reason Mr Doyle had to get a pacemaker fitted.

Mr Doyle had been sitting in his car talking on his phone when Ned had come galloping straight for him on one of his horses. I'd seen it while I was parking my bike. Mr Doyle turned his head and his eyes got very big and round and his eyebrows darted high up his forehead.

It probably would have been a shocking thing to see anyone galloping at full speed – in the exact direction of your car – even if you didn't happen to be sitting in the driver's seat at the time. Sometimes I still think about the expression on Mr Doyle's astonished face as Ned got closer.

'Stop that boy!' shouted Mr Carmody, our principal, who was running, waving his arms around like a cartoon character, as Ned took off again. There'd been no stopping Ned, though. When he was on his horse, he had rules of his own. Nobody could stop him.

So then Mr Carmody rushed over to Mr Doyle, who had frozen inside his car like a picture, his hands gripping the steering wheel as if they'd been stuck with glue.

'This definitely means trouble for Ned Buckley,' Mr Carmody had said grimly as he came into our classroom.

'Good luck with that,' whispered Brendan, whose dad already had a theory that Ned was a lawless boy with no respect for anything or anyone.

I dreamed of Ned a few times after that and in my dreams he was on his horse, galloping in slow motion, just as I'd seen him, just as everyone had, his dark eyes looking at me as he passed, with Mr Doyle staring in his car and everyone else with pale, stunned faces looking on.

Mr Carmody seemed suddenly keen to point out that Mr Doyle had had an underlying heart problem for years and that his hospitalisation didn't have anything to do with Ned, and furthermore, that it was dangerous to suggest otherwise, because that gave some sort of power to Ned that they didn't think he deserved. Teachers have their reputations to protect. Dougie reckoned Mr Doyle didn't want anybody thinking he was a wimp.

And besides, according to most of our teachers, you're not supposed to give power to wild boys on horses. It only encourages them.

5

Serena was on Ned Buckley's side from the start, which was lucky for him, because, even though they pretended to be, none of the other teachers were. There were lots of reasons why Serena was different from the rest of them.

When once we asked her what she was doing in Ireland, she said she'd come for love, which was, she said, a very common reason for a lot of people going anywhere.

She was from a town in Northern Italy where the sun never stopped shining. We wondered how she put up with the glumness of rainy Ballyross. Our other teachers had bobbles on their jumpers and thin greying scarves and sensible shoes. She wore flawless suits made of cashmere sent over from a Tuscan tailor. Other teachers would say things about her once in a while, like they had no idea how the heels she wore didn't give her bunions, or where she found the time to do her hair in the mornings. Apart from a silver stripe along the middle, her hair was glossy black. Her voice had a fizz and a crackle, like a firework.

She drove an old red Italian car that sounded like a hairdryer.

She said it wasn't her job to be liked. It was her job to teach, and teaching is not a popularity contest. She expected everyone to work hard. There was no excuse, she said, for not doing your best.

She could talk for Ireland about the early settlers, and the 1916 rising, and the inauguration of Mary Robinson. And when she talked about those things it never seemed endless or boring.

She told us to call her by her first name. She said she was the member of a noble, ancient family.

When it comes to what you want people to think of you, she told us once, nothing matters quite as much as *La Bella Figura* – which is not so much about looking beautiful as it is about the way you walk into a room.

When Serena walked into our classroom, everything sparkled for a moment: the tips of our pencils; the buckles on our bags; the normally-dull-brown clips in Orla Mulvey's hair. Serena would place her pile of books and notebooks on the table, business-like and determined.

'Students, you're loitering,' she said one day after she'd met us in the corridor. 'There's going to be a lightning strike exam very shortly. You should be making use of this time to study.'

When she said 'lightning strike exam' she actually

meant 'spot test' but Serena had a different way of saying things.

'Sorry, Serena,' we said together and dashed away in different directions as if we had somewhere important to go.

It was Serena who didn't think we should listen to Brendan or anyone else about people's reputations. She thought everyone should make up their own minds, and Laura and Dougie and I agreed.

'We should try to make friends with Ned,' Laura said.

'How do you know he even *wants* to be friends with us?' I asked on the outdoor benches over lunch. The air was practically white with cold. Dougie's breath came out in puffs of fog, and Laura's nose was red.

'He's pretty interested in you,' said Laura in the sing-song voice she uses when she's trying to torment me.

'He is not!' I said, feeling my face heat up.

'She's right, Minty,' said Dougie. 'It might seem like he never takes any notice of anyone – but he's always looking at you.'

'Shut up,' I said, and I pushed Dougie, but only gently, just to make a point.

Dougie pushed me back so hard I fell off the end of the bench.

We told Dougie he'd be the perfect person to ask Ned if he wanted to hang out with us after school. Dougie's kindness was legendary. We thought it would be just the thing to hook Ned in.

Laura and I hovered by the lockers as Dougie asked.

'Thanks, but nah,' is what Ned said in reply.

'No worries, Ned, that's OK,' Dougie answered – and for more proof that Ned's refusal hadn't caused any hard feelings, Laura stepped forward and held out her hand. That didn't go too well either. Ned just looked at her for a tiny second, saying nothing. He turned and walked away, leaving Laura with her hand still sticking out in front of her.

It wasn't easy to become friends with Ned Buckley. As well as not talking, he didn't always come to school and when he did, everyone felt more comfortable avoiding him. The teachers didn't ask him questions, though they had no problem interrogating the rest of us to within an inch of our lives about a whole load of random things to do with rock formations and Hamlet's motives, and where chlorophyll can be found.

I used to wonder where Ned was when he didn't show up while the rest of us were stuck in school, getting ready for lightning strike exams. I imagined him and his horses and reckoned that they were the reason why he stayed away.

I was never allowed to have anything to do with horses, even though I loved them. For my whole life, I hadn't even been allowed to pat one. Mum is allergic and she blows up like a balloon if she even looks at a horse. So I was sort of jealous of Ned. But it wasn't just to do with his horses – it was more about a different kind of freedom that belonged to him, the way he didn't feel the pressure to have to be nice to anyone or to speak when he didn't feel like speaking or to smile when he didn't feel like smiling.

I, on the other hand, had to do loads of things I didn't want to. Mum was forever telling me to look cheerful and I was forever doing my best even when I totally did not feel like it.

Everywhere, people around me spend their lives pretending to feel things that they don't feel. Ned was different. He may not have said much, but it felt like he was always being true and honest, and it felt like he was never pretending to be something he wasn't, or to feel something he didn't feel, or say something he didn't want to say. I wished I could be more like that.

You might have expected me to get the message and stay away, but I wanted to believe that Laura and Dougie had been right. Maybe Ned *had* been looking at me. Maybe there was a chance that I could make a connection with him.

It was that hope, I guess, that made me start going back to Nettlebog on my own. I'd promised Dougie and Laura not to go there without them, but there were things even they didn't understand. And though I felt kind of guilty about going alone, the place gave me a feeling I needed.

When it was dry, I could lie on the mossy ground, springy as a mattress. If it rained I could shelter in the dark bushes and not get even slightly wet. At night, there was a shimmer that felt unreal, as if I was on another planet maybe, or inside a dream. When the sun shone, rays spiked through the branches like things you could hold in your hand. And the whole time there was the black river making gentle noises, so high sometimes that I didn't know where it started and where the shore ended. So low at other times that I could see twisted tree roots, and the handlebars and wheels of a mangled dead bicycle that had become fossilised and fused like buried treasure. I plucked shining coloured stones out of the silt and slid them into my pocket to look at later, when I was away from Nettlebog and supposed to be thinking about other stuff.

I still went there with Laura and Dougie too, but I didn't tell them about my own secret visits. It had been Laura's idea to take rags whenever we went to Nettlebog together, so we could wipe the evidence, the silt and mud, off our tyres before we got home. Parents go insane when you come in with muddy bikes. They say stuff like, 'You've been down that lane again, haven't you?' and you end up having to say things like, 'I wasn't anywhere near the place', making sure your voice sounds scandalised at the very suggestion.

Nettlebog made us watchful, and we noticed things: like how sloppy and squelchy Nettlebog mud can be; like how little waves came in silky ripples, and stained the coloured stones to deeper shades. Like how there are jagged rocks everywhere, which we had to look out for, and how on higher ground, a breeze often shivered through the bushes as if there were nervous, sneaky animals hiding there.

Apart from the thick green bunch of trees that huddled at the edge, the other trees were crooked and contorted, reaching from the ground, their bent branch-fingers scarring the sky.

The river was often rough, and at night the water was dark and inky. Thick like oil. Ghostly shapes slipped in and out of sight behind the trunks and branches. Every time I went down there, it seemed as if there were a thousand things I hadn't seen before.

Sometimes the river was a mirror and sometimes it was a window. One moment it looked smooth enough to walk on. And then next thing, it was stippled and crusty, like the skin of some massive reptile, alive and breathing. There were so many things about it that I couldn't know and when I think about it, I could say the same about Ned, who was part of that place, who slept and woke in the reflection of the shiny strange amazingness of it all.

Whenever I was there I felt a strange jumble of peace and uneasiness, excitement and fear.

It was impossible to stay away.

Dad was the one who especially didn't want me going there.

But he moved out on the nineteenth of March, which was the day I personally reckon he gave up his right to tell me what I could and couldn't do, and where I could and couldn't go.

The nineteenth of March was the day after my birthday. If that was the reason he'd waited, honestly, he shouldn't have bothered. He spent most of the time packing stuff into suitcases and trying not to be in the same room as Mum. And now when I think about it, what I can remember is both of them walking in and very quickly out of the different rooms in our house as if we were in the middle of a bad play.

I'd begun to be convinced that if I could get to know Ned a bit better, there'd be lots of other things I'd understand too. I held on to the memory of the few times I'd heard his voice, slow and certain, and the way he had looked strong and proud when he'd spoken to Brendan in class and how careless he'd seemed when he'd refused our hand

22

of friendship and how wild and sort of lovely he'd looked galloping on the horse with the reddish brown coat like a conker, the black mane and four white feet.

As a matter of fact, I couldn't get Ned out of my head. The boy who lived in a caravan. The boy who owned two horses. The boy who lit midnight bonfires and who swung over and back above the river, bellowing loud, unfathomable things. That boy who everybody said was no good.

6

My parents could have told me that something was wrong. It's not like I didn't know. There were plenty of signs: silent breakfasts in the kitchen, gritted teeth at the front door. Seething whispers on the landing.

They did try to smile at each other sometimes, but I had grown quite good at telling the difference between genuine smiles and joyless grins. Gradually, even the grinning disappeared.

Soon there was mostly nothing between them except sourness and anger – squeezed into every word and every glance, bursting to get out. Whenever they spoke to each other it felt as if there was something escaping into the air, like poisonous gas leaking from invisible cracks: colourless and difficult to name – but deadly all the same.

If I'm honest, things had been going wrong for a while. One day Mum was sorting through old files and papers in the back room, when Dad went in to look for something. He left the door open. It didn't take long before I could hear them talking in their horrible low-voiced way. Mum threw this massive pack of photos at my dad. He stood there completely still, with his teeth clamped tight together as the pictures fluttered down around him.

If either of them had turned around at that moment, they'd have seen me staring at them, which would obviously have made everything even worse, so I just rushed up to bed, and dived under my duvet, breathing fast, feeling as if *I* was the one who'd done something wrong.

When Dad came in to say goodnight, he looked like he'd been for a run. A bead of sweat was sliding down the side of his face.

'What's up?' I asked.

'Look, love,' he sighed, 'there's an issue, OK, but it's between your mother and me, so I can't . . . I just can't . . .'

Dad was sad and crumpled and I could see his chin wobbling. So, I did what I always do when things between me and Dad get awkward: I tried to lighten the mood.

'Whoa, Dad, come on. Hey! Cool your jets!'

Cool your jets might sound a really silly sort of thing to say, but it used to be me and my dad's catchphrase. For some reason, he used to say it to me a lot when I was smaller. We both used to think it was pretty funny. It's good to have a fail-safe thing to say in sticky situations, and I was glad of it right then because it made him laugh, just like it always had.

Nobody sat me down the way they do in the movies. Nobody explained anything to me, or updated me on the things that were going on between Mum and Dad. Whenever I tried to talk about it, they kept repeating how it was just between them and how they were working hard not to involve me, or to let it affect me.

But when the members of your family are in grim moods for months on end – well, I'm sorry to break it to you – but it is your business – it's got everything to do with you – and someone should have the decency to let you know.

Not that I wasn't figuring it out by myself. It's not as if I had to be Sherlock Holmes or anything.

It got so as just coming in the door of our house made me feel as if someone was sitting on my chest, trying to crush the breath out of me. I used to open the windows to try to get a breeze blowing through as if that was going to get rid of the deadness and the bitterness and the silence and the regret.

And anyway, Mum and Dad would go round closing them wondering why I was trying to heat the outside world, and asking me if I was under the false impression they were made of money.

So then Mum's phone rang one day, and she screwed up her mouth with something that looked like a mixture of anger and sadness. She hung up and tossed the phone into the bowl in the middle of our kitchen table.

'Who was that?'

Mum dragged the back of her hand across her eyes and gave me one of her pointless, fragile, happiness-free smiles.

'Oh, Minty, it's nothing. Nothing, darling. Don't worry about it.'

I get it. I understand when someone doesn't want to talk and I'm not the kind of person to be pushy about it, so I said OK, and asked her if she fancied a cup of tea, and Mum said that would be lovely.

'Come on,' she said. 'The sun is shining for the first time in ages, and the daffodils have started to poke through and the garden looks like it's waking up. Let's go out and make the most of it.'

The day after that, Dad was late for work. He'd accidentally left his own phone on the kitchen table. It rang three times.

'LINDY' flashed up on the screen with a photo of this beaming blonde woman holding a colossal bunch of flowers.

For someone who never interferes in anyone else's business, it's surprising how hard I find it to let a phone keep on ringing, especially when it's bleating away in front of me. So on the fourth time, I snapped.

'Richard Malone's daughter,' I said in a fake official voice that I enjoy using from time to time.

But just then, Dad burst back in through the door like an explosion.

'For goodness sake, Minty,' he yelled. 'Will you stop messing and GIVE that BACK to me?'

He acted as if I'd gone out of my way to take his phone, as if I'd stolen it or something – as if it wasn't him in his fog of distraction who'd been careless enough to leave it behind.

'I NEED it!' He grabbed it out of my hand, shoved it into his coat pocket and left again. For all I know, the person who was ringing could have been on the line the whole time, listening to him going crazy about nothing.

I wanted to run out after him and shout. I wanted him to know that, for his information, he was nothing more than a rude, grumpy old man. But instead I did what mature grown-ups do when they are angry about something, I sent him a text.

'It wasn't my fault you left your stupid phone behind. I was only trying to help.'

'Sorry, love. Things a bit stressful. Rushed. Love you. Sad.'

Had he meant to text 'Dad' or was he filling me in on his current emotional state? Either way, I was glad that he'd had the decency to apologise.

When I was very young, my parents put glow-in-the-dark stickers of the planets on the ceiling of my bedroom. In the old days, it was soothing to look at them. They filled me with wonder. But lately when I lay awake looking at them, they reminded me of things I didn't want to think about. How Mum and Dad had been happy when they put them there, and how one day, I don't know exactly when, they just stopped being. Their fake lights were no comfort to me, not the way they used to be. Not any more.

Dad's apologetic mood didn't last very long. He was chopping the onions for dinner and I was laying the table when I decided to ask, 'Who's Lindy?'

Dad's hand slipped. He cut his finger quite badly.

I had to look in about fifty different places for a bandage and Dad stood in the middle of the kitchen with blood plopping onto the tiles. According to him it was all my fault for distracting him.

Secrets in a family can make you feel a bit like there's someone inside your head in a big rage, throwing heavy things around.

It was good when Saturday morning came. Dad left early to play tennis with his boss, and Mum went off to Pilates. I didn't have much time to enjoy the silence and peace, though, because not long after the stillness had settled, the doorbell rang.

It was the real-life Lindy. It took me a second or two before I realised where I'd seen her face before – staring at me from my dad's phone with 'LINDY' flashing on and off.

I told her Dad was out, and she said she knew he was, and that it wasn't my dad she was looking for. It was my mum she wanted to talk to.

'Sorry,' I said. 'No can do. Out too. You'll have to make do with me.'

She looked thoughtful for a moment and then she said, 'Listen, I know this is a difficult situation and everything, but your father deserves to be happy.'

Everyone deserves to be happy, not just my dad, is what I realised I should have said – but I didn't think of that until much later, way after she'd left.

'OK then, can you please tell your mother that I called and that I'd like to talk to her.'

'You can say anything you want to me. I'm perfectly capable of passing on a message.'

She said no, she'd prefer not to, thanks all the same.

'OK, can I tell my mum what this is in connection with?'

'She probably knows already,' said Lindy, and she twirled around and skipped down to our gate in her flat golden shoes and her floaty white skirt and her tanned skin.

7

When Dad finally got round to telling me he was leaving it didn't come as a massive surprise.

He made his announcement the day before my birthday and he left the day after, so needless to say, those three days were a non-stop, full-on, laugh-a-minute.

Afterwards, the only thing Mum kept on saying was how important it was to be cheerful.

So I would lock the door of my room and walk slowly over to the corner and get down on my knees. Then I would curl up very small and I would do this silent wail with tears falling sideways into my ear, and I would stay there doing that for a while, and then I would get up and wipe my face and brush my hair and straighten myself out and unlock the door and pretend that I hadn't even been crying.

Happy isn't something that happens to you, Mum would repeat.

'No kidding,' I'd reply.

'Of course not. You see, happy is something you choose to be.'

'Take me for example, Minty, I mean I could easily be down in the dumps about, you know . . . about a great deal of different things these days . . . but you see I'm just not letting the situation get to me. I refuse. Guess why? Because I've *chosen* to be happy.'

I wasn't going to argue with her. Even though it was obvious she was lying her head off.

'We're fine!' she'd say to anyone who even looked as if they were going to ask her about how we were. She claimed that the whole scenario was just an example of experienced grown-ups moving on with their lives. For everyone's sake apparently, she and Dad had resolved to remain on friendly terms.

Friendly terms? Seriously? They hadn't been on friendly terms for ages.

'Let's not bother with the ins and outs of it if anyone asks,' she suggested.

'No point dwelling on the past' and 'We are where we are' became her sayings of the season.

She didn't realise how crazy she looked with her fake cheerfulness, acting like everything was OK and as if she had a brilliant new attitude to everything. It made her talk differently and it made her smile the bizarre wide-looking smile that was beginning to drive me mad.

'I'm going to make sure you and I have the best year ever,' she declared, as if I was a little kid, and as if I didn't know how watchful and edgy she was.

And then it seemed as if Mum was gripped with a new and terrible energy. In a single day, she cleaned everything out of the cupboards in the utility room and she scrubbed the kitchen floor and she polished the bath and painted the front door, and climbed up the step-ladder so she could take down the curtains in the living room because she thought they were filthy. After they were washed and dried, she ironed them and put them back up again.

'Honestly, Mum, this can't go on,' I said.

'What can't?' she asked, sounding mystified.

'The demented cleaning,' I replied. 'The pretend joy.'

'Don't be silly,' said Mum. 'What this is, is a positive attitude, which by the way, darling, is what we both need. A decent clean. A fresh start. Just the things to clear our heads and pave the way for a whole new chapter in our lives.'

'I don't want a new chapter. I want the old chapter. The one where the three of us were together. The one before Dad had a woman called Lindy in his phone.'

'Lindy?' said my mum, putting the iron down in slow motion, and settling warily into the armchair. 'You know about Lindy?'

'Ya, I know about her. She dropped by. I've had a conversation with her.'

'She came *here*? She called to the house?'

'Yes.'

'When?'

'About a month ago.'

'A *month* ago? Why didn't you tell me?'

'I'm telling you now.'

'What does she look like?'

'She looks young.'

As soon as I said it, I realised it was totally the wrong thing to say.

Next thing there was a big green rubbish skip outside with about a hundred and fifty of my dad's things in it. From my window I could see the steely rims of his drum kit flashing in the sunshine beside a broken rake. A poster of him and the members of his old band was nesting in a bed of shirts next to a multi-coloured flock of ties.

Dad rang to say he was going to drop by to collect some more of his stuff.

'I should warn you, Dad, Mum's spring cleaning. There's a skip.'

When he arrived he hammered on the door and shouted at Mum and Mum said don't you dare put a foot in this house, or so help me . . . and Dad said, what . . . what will you do? And she said, are you threatening me?

And he said it was she who was threatening him.

I think the shouting must have gone on for a long time after that, but it was right around then that I left and headed to the archway of Nettlebog. I ran fast down the whole of the lane until I felt far away, until I was next to the water, until I'd breathed in the Nettlebog smell and felt the Nettlebog feeling.

I sat so close that my feet got wet and I put my head on my knees and I cried a proper loud, sobby cry. It felt horrible but it also felt a lot better than the strangled tears behind the door of my room.

It wasn't until I heard a rustle that I realised someone was there.

'Oh, hello, lovey. Hello. I hope you don't mind me asking, but what's wrong?'

I guess I should have wiped my face and made my excuses. It had been a long time though, since anyone had asked me what was wrong. It had been a long time since anyone seemed to have noticed anything about me at all.

Her face was calm and kind. She wore a purple velvet skirt which looked like a curtain, that went right down to her feet and she had a pale green apron on, and her hair was pure white. There was no reason for her to ask me what was wrong but she had and her voice was deep, and it had sounded so true and kind and I couldn't help myself.

'Everything is a lie,' I told her.

'Is it now?' she asked. 'And how do you make that out?'

'There is a skip outside my house, and there was a time when I thought every single thing in it meant something important to my parents but they are screaming at each other on the street by our front door. My dad's drums, and his ties, and the pictures of their wedding, and books they bought for each other as presents. Now each of those things tells a story, a bad story. The story of a lie. A skip full of lies.

'And my mum's been trying to act as if there's nothing wrong and that we are perfectly happy and that there's nothing to be sad about.

'And I'm beginning to realise the human race is nothing but millions of liars – doing nothing but lying to each other and to themselves, and I'm sick of it and it just makes me so . . . so mad. But there's nothing I can do because I'm stuck. Stuck here in a trap full of lies.'

She didn't overreact like a lot of people might have when they saw someone ranting and crying. And in the middle of her old face, her eyes looked young and they were shining. I kept crying and she kept being calm.

'Ah, dear,' she said. 'You poor girl.'

'I'm sorry.' I sniffed.

'What are you sorry for? Isn't this exactly what you need to be doing, and isn't this the perfect place to do it, away from that noise and the bother you've run from? And aren't you very wise to be taking a break from it?'

It's unusual to say so much to someone you've only

just met. Eventually, she said I'd be more than welcome to come into her caravan, which is when I began to think that she must be something to do with Ned, but I was too timid to ask, so I said no I'd been enough trouble already, and she shook her head and smiled and said I hadn't been the slightest bit of trouble. She said I probably didn't even know the meaning of the word.

We talked a bit more. She wasn't sure how useful it would be, but she said she had some advice.

'There's a general theory in life that lies are bad,' she said, 'but not all of them are. Sometimes we need them.'

I said I didn't understand what she meant and then she said. 'Ah, well, you see now, that's the great thing about life, you don't have to understand everything in one go. You will when the time is right. When you're ready. Life is long. You don't have to be in too much of a hurry to get a handle on every bit of it at the same time.'

She said I might know her grandson, Ned Buckley.

I should have known, I supposed, I mean part of me had guessed already, so I wasn't so surprised, but still it sort of felt like gigantic news too: this woman who had found me here – and who she was connected to.

'You're Ned's gran?'

'I am indeed, lovey.'

'Wow. I mean, goodness me. I mean, cool.'

Then, for no reason I could understand, I felt myself going red, and I could feel myself hoping she wasn't going to notice.

'I'm in his class,' I told her.

'Oh, for goodness sake,' she chuckled. 'Isn't it a small world?'

I asked her not to say anything to Ned about meeting me, and not to tell him about what a basketcase I'd been. She said she wouldn't dream of telling him any such thing.

'Don't suppose he says much at school,' she said, and I said no, not much. I told her I thought he might have settled in a bit better if his friend Martin Cassidy hadn't dropped out.

'Martin Cassidy?' she said. 'His friend?'

She laughed and I asked her what was funny, and she said you could say a lot about them, but you could never call them friends.

I said something like, 'Wow, I'd never have guessed that,' and she suggested that the reason I didn't see it was maybe I hadn't looked closely enough. She said she wasn't surprised that Martin had left, and I said why, and she said some things in life were very hard, and among the hardest thing in the whole world was the prospect of keeping boys like Martin and Ned at school.

'I imagine you don't see Ned every day. I'd say he struggles a bit to keep up with the lessons.'

Her eyes twinkled and I wasn't sure what to say, so I didn't say anything. I thought maybe I'd get Ned into trouble. But she said, don't worry, I know him inside out and I don't bother about the things he does and the places he goes. He has quite a lot going on.

'My darling Ned has a lot of rivers to cross,' is how

she put it and I loved the sound of Ned being a darling –
cherished by someone who seemed full of wisdom.

'I don't force him to go, but I think in the long run it's
doing him good. I never got an education myself and as
old as I am, I still regret it. He has to do it by himself,
though. Forcing anyone to go to school defeats the
purpose,' she said. 'And you see, he's very busy these days
because of the training.'

'Training? For what?'

'For the Ballyross Race.'

She seemed surprised I'd never heard of it. She said it
was famous. She said it was one of the reasons that she
and Ned had come back here. This is where her son had
grown up, and he'd ridden in the race a long time ago.
Now it was Ned's turn.

The Ballyross Race happens every year in a great
empty field beside the old factory across the river. Riders
compete on horses with no saddles. It takes a lot of skill.
It was the main reason Martin and Ned were not friends,
but enemies. They were both getting ready for it this year.
Ned had never beaten him. 'It's driving him daft,' she said.

I thought about Ned leaping and twisting and galloping.
None of the wonderful things she kept saying about him
were surprising.

'Between ourselves,' she said, 'Ned's been working
hard. He's in with a very good chance this year. But don't
tell anyone. He's the dark horse.'

'What's a dark horse?'

'Someone who stays quiet about themselves but who's

gradually getting themselves ready to dazzle the world in the end.'

'Oh, right,' I said.

We chatted for quite a long time. I asked her if it was just she and Ned who lived at Nettlebog and she said yes. She'd once had an enormous family but most of them were dead or gone. There was Ned's great aunt, her sister, who was still around, living in Kerry. She visited her a lot but it was getting harder to bring Ned these days on account of him not wanting to leave the horses.

I explained how much I loved horses and about how annoyed I was with my mum for having allergies. She declared that allergies aren't technically someone's fault and I said OK I suppose she had a point. I told her that this might be a good chance for me to hang out with horses, that I'd be happy to take care of them or give her a hand if ever she needed me to, and she said that was a very kind offer, and she'd keep it in mind. She said she'd be even happier if I'd offered to take care of Ned, because he was the one that needed most taking care of. We both had a laugh about that.

I asked her where Ned was now and she said off perfecting his turns for the Ballyross, but that his other horse was in the shed if I'd like to come and see her. I said I'd love to and she handed me a stick, and it was useful for tramping along the bumpy ground. Phoebe was the name of the horse and she was one single colour, pale, beautiful grey with eyes of black. She was so beautiful that I couldn't even pat her on the head. I could hardly look at her. For some reason, looking at her this close up made me want to cry.

By the time I said goodbye to Ned's gran and made my rocky way back along Nettlebog Lane, I'd nearly forgotten about Mum and Dad and Lindy and the skip and the fighting, but I knew those things would be still there, waiting for me when I got back.

Mum was getting worse. You could tell because of the way she kept starting new things and how everything about her felt entirely random and unpredictable. When I came home from school there was no knowing what she'd be up to. I'd find her writing furiously in a golden-covered notebook, or planting garlic in the garden or knitting. She'd taken out subscriptions for three different kinds of self-help magazines called 'You Can Heal Your Life!' and 'Starting Over' and 'Moving On – A Guide for Women'. It was completely out of character. Worst of all, she was becoming a vegan. The only things in our cupboards were cans of coconut milk, and the only things in our fridge were soft blocks of tofu.

41

'It's a total lifestyle transformation!' she beamed, plonking a plate of brown rice and kidney beans in front of me. I told her I had no interest in being a vegan and that from now on I'd make my own plans for dinner.

8

If *I'd* ever had the nerve to miss as much as five *minutes* of school, I know exactly what would happen: there'd be a load of conferences and cardiac arrests and serious-faced discussions and my parents would probably put aside their differences so they could come into the school together. And then there'd be a whole series of talks with my teachers and my parents would instantly take the side of the teachers, regardless of whether or not I had a good explanation.

It was unfair, thinking about it, that Ned, on the other hand, could disappear for days on end, and how none of the teachers did anything much except a bit of extra record-keeping and some sighing and eye-rolling.

Mum said Ned's absence was the sign of a lot of sad things – all based on a life of chaos, probably. But I knew better. He was practising skills for something bigger and greater and more important than anything he was ever going to be asked to do at school.

Maybe it was the things his gran had said about him but whatever the reason, Ned had begun drifting into my head more and more – and there didn't seem to be anything I could do to stop him. There were things about him that I missed when he wasn't around. I missed the way he swaggered into class. I missed the silent look in his eyes. I missed the idea that Dougie and Laura had given me that maybe when I wasn't looking at him, he was looking at me.

'Does anyone else wonder where he is?' I asked and Dougie said to be honest, he hadn't even noticed Ned was absent.

'Hello? We're busy. Serena's setting us another one of her lightning strike exams. We need to be ready,' he said. 'There isn't that much time to sit around worrying whether certain people are at school or not.'

I imagined some of the things Ned must be doing while we were stuck in class. I pictured his big brown horse with the white feet, and I pictured Phoebe, the smaller one of the softest grey and her black eyes and her eyelashes and how she'd felt too beautiful for me to touch. I pictured Ned training for the race, or minding his gorgeous horses or galloping around the place for no reason except because he could. And I began to understand the things about him that nobody else seemed to have seen. The things that were hidden. The things that were secret. The things that were kind of rich.

Just when everyone thought Ned was never coming back, he strolled in without even a murmur of apology, and definitely without an explanation, acting as if he'd never been gone. He had a brand new leather jacket and shoes I hadn't seen before.

I have learned that when someone stays away from school for big stretches of time, and when someone is as different and separate as Ned always was in those days, something else happens. Everyone begins to act strangely around them and this is what began to happen whenever Ned showed up.

Any time he walked into class, Brendan would cough this fake cough and then some of the others, including Laura and Dougie and I, would laugh.

We knew Ned didn't care about what anyone else did or what they said, or the noises they made, or whether they laughed or who they laughed at. That kind of stuff was irrelevant to him.

I watched him when he sat down, squashing his knees underneath his desk. He stared out of the window like he always did, humming gentle and low to himself as if he wasn't even *in* school.

He took off the jacket and it fell onto the floor in a soft leathery mound behind his chair. He closed his eyes for a second or so.

And we stared and some of us glared and Brendan made sputtering neighing noises, as if he was trying to sound like a horse, but Ned didn't look over and he didn't laugh or frown or do anything in response.

Not long after those kinds of things had started, Serena came to the locker room and said Dougie and Laura and I were to follow her, and the three of us walked behind her to the staff room, making big round-eyed faces at each other and asking in whispers if any of us had any clue what we were supposed to have done wrong.

'Mr Carmody tells me that he has recently noticed a mood growing in your class. A mood of sneering. A mood of jeering.'

The three of us stood there, with only a slight idea what she was talking about.

'Within these four walls – and I would not normally discuss other students in this way – I do want you to know that it has taken a lot to get Ned Buckley to keep coming to school. I need you to know how important it is for him to be here – and how essential it is that nobody puts him off, accidentally or on purpose.

'I do not think that you are bad students and I see no malice in your spirits, but I would like to make a particular point about what you need to be conscious of – about what I am going to say – you need to do everything in your power to be *simpatico* to Ned Buckley.'

'*Simpatico*?' Dougie mouthed at me and I shrugged.

'His life isn't as easy as yours,' she said, 'and you should keep that in mind.'

'Not as *easy* as *ours*?' Dougie said to me in a scandalised voice, after Serena had let us out. 'He hardly ever comes to school. His entire life hasn't been basically *squandered* on organised education. He gets to come and go as he pleases. He flies around the place *on a horse*. That he *owns*.'

I thought about Nettlebog Lane and its archway made out of trees. And I thought again how the spirit of the place lingered around Ned wherever he went and I thought about how strange it felt sometimes, to have a place like that right beside the ordinary places in my life, and a person like Ned, living right next to me. But he might as well have been on another planet considering how far away from me he always felt.

We tried to start more conversations with Ned after that but somehow during those few weeks, he had become even more of an island. He would sit in the same corner near the window, leaning back and staring into the distance, thinking about some big plan that didn't involve us. And I guessed that part of that plan was probably to do with figuring out how he was going to beat Martin Cassidy in the race.

And he kept on not looking at anyone and not talking. And at the end of each day, he always did that thing where he pushed his chair with the back of his legs, and you could hear the chair scraping along the wooden floor before he walked out.

'He's in trouble with the council for riding around on those horses like some lunatic,' explained Brendan.

'He doesn't have a licence,' added Laura.

'Who?' I said. 'Who are you talking about?'

'Who do you think? Ned Buckley.'

'And who has been saying those things? Who told you stuff like that about him?'

'Lots of people,' said Brendan.

'You've got to admit he's not normal,' added Laura. 'You must have an idea about how strange he is.'

'His grandmother has no teeth and she has witchy white hair that spikes out, and a crooked stick.'

'Oh, does she, now?' And something inside me tightened like a screw.

'Yeah, she waves it around in the air whenever strangers come too near. And you should see the state of the banged-up old rust bucket she drives around the place in.'

'I've met her,' I told them. 'She has plenty of teeth and her hair is not in the slightest bit witchy. And I've never seen her waving sticks in the air. She uses them to walk around. Nettlebog is very rocky by the bank, and she's quite old. She needs to watch her step. And so what if her car's a bit battered and wrecked? That's no reason to be mean.

'She's got a gentle voice and she smiles a very nice smile too and her eyes look young. She's kind. She's clever. And she's just decent.'

'OK, maybe, but anyway, I know for a fact,' said Brendan, his voice getting high on its own knowledge, 'the only reason Ned even turns up to school is because of some agreement made with a judge in a court of law.'

If Ned ever had a chance of being anyone's friend, that chance looked like it was vanishing, the way a bird might fly off and disappear behind a mountain.

Of course, as usual, none of this made any difference to him.

Rumours are only words. They move about in the air from one voice to another and they are invisible. Funny to think how powerful they can be all the same – how some can be like knives with sharp edges that can cut, how others are cold hammers – how they can do so much damage, as if they are real, solid objects flying around hitting you in the face when you least expect it.

9

I found divorce papers in the study. I don't know why finding them should have bothered me so much. I mean, I already knew the story with my mum and dad, but somehow looking at those official words, those neat little black marks that were the official end of my parents' togetherness – it was a harsh and lonely moment looking at the truth, spelled out in posh language with lines at the bottom where Mum and Dad had written their signatures. Anyway, the point is, it would have been nice if someone had told me about it. It would have been nice if I didn't have to stumble on it by accident on my own.

Not long after that, Dad phoned pretending that he was interested in how Mum and I were doing when actually what he wanted was to tell me was that he and Lindy were getting married and he wanted me to be a hundred per cent involved. He asked if I would be their flower girl. I said yes, even though flower girls are small children and even though nobody seems to have noticed that I am not a small child.

I wanted to point that out, but by then I'd already calculated the ideal length of my conversations with Dad. Sixty seconds. Max. Any longer than that and he'd always say he had to go. *I* wanted to be the one to go first.

Mum said we had to be happy for him and she did her smile.

'Mum, please don't do this. Please stop pretending to be OK when you're not and when you couldn't possibly be. Remember, I've *seen* the two of you roaring at each other. I've heard the things you've said.'

'Oh, Minty, come on, that was us letting off steam, getting a few things off our chests. That's behind us now.'

'Mum, please. Will you not just talk to *me*? Say something about it.'

'About what?'

I wanted to scream at her. I wanted to stand up and jump around and shout: 'About everything! About how he's let us down and abandoned us and how he's getting on with his new life and we're left here with the dregs of his old one.'

But I couldn't. She had this way of not letting me say those things before I even opened my mouth.

Dad kept on ringing and he made this speech most of which was mainly to do with 'central roles' – how much he was looking forward to me playing a central role in the wedding, and how he had no intention of not playing a central role as my parent just because he didn't live with us; how completely crucial it was that I got to know Lindy better, seeing as she was going to play a central role in my life from now on.

And then straight after that he contradicted himself the way he'd recently got into the habit of doing: he told me that Lindy didn't want there to be any kids at the wedding after eleven, and apparently that included me. I laughed, even though Dad didn't seem to think there was anything ironic about that.

'A totally central role, but just until eleven, is that it, Dad?' I clarified, and he said that was exactly it.

I was going to have to get a lift home with Lindy's grandparents, who were so ancient I was surprised they were even allowed to be in charge of a car.

It wasn't too much of a shock to hear Mum saying that she didn't understand what I was quite so upset about. Eleven was the perfect time to leave a wedding. The best fun of any night has always happened by then. Any time after that, things often go seriously downhill.

It killed me the way Mum kept lying to me. By saying she was happy. By saying she was perfectly fine with this. Pretending that she saw nothing but good in the world, and in other people, and in me.

'Take off your ridiculous mask of happiness, Mum,' I wanted to tell her, as usual. 'Stop this ridiculous act!' I wanted to plead. 'How can you keep making-believe that everything is fine?' I wanted to ask.

But as usual, I said nothing, and I kept the rage inside

me and it was hot and angry and a little bit insane. You'd never have known it from the outside. From the outside it would have been easy to assume I was an ordinary person, calm and normal. Which just goes to show you should never assume anything.

10

For a while afterwards, I thought maybe the closer Dad and Lindy's wedding got, the more likely it might be that Mum would eventually crumble, and that if she did then she and I could have a proper conversation about everything.

I tried some straight talking tactics, as in, 'Mum, you know you can tell me how you're feeling.' But I was no match for Mum, who'd become the complete mistress of blanking me on issues of that nature.

'About what?' she replied.

'About your husband getting married to someone who's not you. About me being his flower girl. About him starting a new life. About you not being invited to the wedding. About your whole world being pulled from under you.'

'Oh, come on now,' she said, pressing her lips together and concentrating more closely on an apparently endless rainbow scarf she was in the middle of knitting. I hoped she didn't think I was going to wear it, but I couldn't imagine who else she might be making it for.

'Sweetheart. My life is going perfectly, in fact, it's going so well that I have some news. I wasn't going to tell you until after you'd come back from Dad and Lindy's do, but it might be just the thing to reassure you . . . to prove to you that I am utterly OK and that I'm getting on fine without your father.'

Mum had got a job in the library. She was going to be going there every Wednesday, Friday and Saturday. She had her own office. Or at least, they'd cleared a beautiful room at the back, overlooking the Ballyross bridge, and they were going to let her use it.

'What will you be doing?' I asked.

'Literacy support in the local community. I'm going to help children who are struggling to read and write. They're letting me design my own sign.'

'And, Minty, guess what the sign says,' she said, looking as if she was about to tell me some massive, wonderful secret.

'What?'

'The Mountain of Knowledge!'

She was grinning now in an unsettling kind of a way, searching my face, waiting for the significance of it to sink in.

It hit me, OK, more or less immediately. Once, when I was about four years old, according to both my parents,

I said 'mountain of knowledge' and apparently that's not an expression and they had thought there was something sweet and comical about me saying it.

'Isn't that a great idea? The librarian said we need to brand this initiative and I was thinking about it in bed the other night and that's when it just came to me. There are quite a few children booked in already.'

'The Mountain of Knowledge?' I repeated.

'Yes, you see, Minty, I think that telling the story of my own daughter's childhood mistake will be the perfect opener for children who are feeling unsure themselves. And now the word is getting round. "Together we can climb the mountain of knowledge: a safe place for anyone who's encountering trouble with their reading or writing," said Mum, sounding as if she was making a formal presentation, or reading from a script.

'I'm going to be helping others to learn. And you know what, Minty? I can feel it building my own confidence again too – getting out there – using my skills outside the home. I can't tell you how much satisfaction and courage it's giving me, to be a force for good in the community. I think this is the beginning of something very special for me.'

I know I should have been happy for her, but I wasn't. I was annoyed, and something inside me suddenly felt like it was breaking.

'The Mountain of Knowledge? Why would you tell that story about me to total strangers, Mum?'

Mum's smile hovered for a moment and then

disappeared. She stopped looking at me and instead stared down at her feet, as she spoke to me, low and solemn.

'It's adorable, Arminta. It's a lovely story. It reminds me of happy times. When you said such funny things.'

'It's not sweet, it's silly. And by the way, for your information, nobody calls me Arminta any more.'

'Why are you being like this?'

'It reminds me of nothing except that babies say stupid things, and just because they do, that's no reason to create a public, permanent reminder of it.'

'Oh, Minty, why are you being so unpleasant, so hurtful? It's not like you, and it doesn't suit you. I thought you'd be pleased for me.'

'Well, I'm not pleased. You never tell me anything until it's too late. Starting a job? Like, you know? That's a terribly big commitment. And it just could have been one of those many things you might actually have thought about discussing with me if you even cared vaguely about how I feel or what I think. I mean, Mum, that's a massive change in our life circumstances. Don't you think there have been enough changes around here to be getting on with? Don't you think we have enough things to adjust to for the moment, thanks very much?'

'I see,' she said, reforming her face into the annoyingly calm expression she was so good at these days – the expression that was driving me crazy.

'It's not about the sign or the story, is it? It's about other things. I have to try to understand why you are acting

57

like this. It's so not you, Minty. You're never selfish. You're hardly ever angry.'

But I *was* selfish and angry. And I was annoyed and raging with her and with Dad and with everyone. In the end Mum said she was sorry, that she should of course have talked to me first, but that she deserved to be getting on with things and she wasn't going to feel bad for making proactive decisions about her own future.

'OK then, just promise me you'll take the sign down, Mum.' And Mum made a promise – which would have been nice of her except that I found out later that she didn't keep it, so she might as well not have bothered to say anything.

That might have been the moment for the two of us to have a proper talk maybe – or at least to stop fighting and tell each other things that were true.

But in my family, we hardly ever do what we are supposed to do.

In fact, right after that, we stopped talking to each other altogether.

11

Two days of silence later, it was Mum who broke the ice by making me some hot chocolate and saying, 'Come on, Minty, I hate when we're not talking. There's nothing I hate more.'

'Let's be friends again,' she said and I said OK to that even though as far as I'm concerned you can't actually be friends with your mother especially when she spends practically the whole time lying – to herself and to everyone else.

When the day of Dad and Lindy's wedding finally came, Mum blow-dried my hair straight like I asked her, and she put flowery clips in and tied the ribbony belt around my waist. I hardly recognised myself.

'I hope you know it's bad manners to look nicer than the bride,' she said.

She told me to be sure to take lots of photos.

'I would very much like them to be happy,' she said, glancing out of the window.

And later, as she was waving me off, she said, 'I wonder how she feels today. I wonder if she knows what she's doing.'

I guessed she was talking about Lindy, but I didn't ask because I didn't want a conversation about what Lindy knew or what she thought or how she felt – I wanted a conversation about how Mum and me felt, but apparently that wasn't allowed. And anyway I had begun to worry that Lindy's parents were about to arrive and I didn't want us to be talking about anything like that when they did.

Lindy turned up in a shimmering white dress with an embroidered bodice. She had fresh petals and pearls in her hair and three glamorous bridesmaids who I'd never met. They wore silk of a pink so faint it could have been white too, and Jez – who played guitar in Dad's band – was best man and he had blue violets in his lapel. My dress looked totally out of place. It didn't go with anything.

Dad's friends kept shifting around in the church, loosening their ties and Jez's shirt looked like it needed to be tucked in. I'd never seen any of Dad's old crew in suits before and it looked as if they'd borrowed them because in some cases the suits were much too big and in Phil's particular case, his trouser legs were flapping around above his ankles so you could see he was wearing odd socks.

On the other side of the church were Lindy's friends and family who looked like movie stars, in dark glasses and perfect make up and magnificent hats.

There had been lots of unexpected things to do when it came to being flower girl. Partly it involved wearing that out-of-place shiny purple dress with a wide black satin belt and partly it meant showing guests to their seats and mainly it involved behaving as if I was having the most ecstatic time of my life.

Everyone did say I looked brilliant, even though I couldn't imagine for a moment they were telling me the truth.

Jez claimed he'd hardly have recognised me and went on about how Dad must be proud, and Dad's other friend Phil asked how Mum was and I said,

'She's fine, perfectly fine, what else would she be?'

And he said, 'Right then, that's great of course, super, I wouldn't have expected otherwise.'

I took a photo of Lindy, whose teeth are very white, but I deleted it straightaway because even though Mum had said to take loads of photos, Lindy looked even younger and happier and more dazzling than usual, and I had this feeling that I didn't want Mum to see that much gorgeousness.

It turns out that it's impossible to take a bad photograph

of Lindy. And for Mum's sake, it wasn't as if I didn't try. Even on the dance floor when everyone else looked sweaty and mad, all Lindy did was shine.

On the up side, she wasn't going to be young for ever – Mum had said before I left – especially considering that she was going to be married to my dad.

Dad was young and happy-looking too.

I took photos of the food.

'Stop messing with your phone, and come and dance with me,' said Dad with proper happiness on his face that made me feel good and guilty at the same time.

And me and Lindy and Dad danced in a circle and everybody clapped like this was a nice thing for us to be doing but, to be honest, I felt stupid, and besides, the ribbon on my dress had started to feel uncomfortable, cutting into me, and I wanted to change because I didn't feel myself any more.

The music was that glad kind that makes everyone want to sing. Gerry and Phil and Jez played loud and joyful and I wanted to take a photo of the three of them with my dad. But at the last minute Lindy photo-bombed the shot by leaping in front of everyone and putting her face close up and her arms spread out. She was trying to be funny and friendly, I guess, but she totally ruined the picture.

You can't exactly tell the bride she's not supposed to be in a photo at her own wedding. That would have sounded kind of crazy and definitely a bit rude.

They sent me home with Lindy's grandparents at eleven o'clock like they said they were going to, and completely contrary to what Mum had predicted, it actually seemed as if the best part of the night was just beginning.

I had the key to our front door on a chain around my neck and I pulled it out when Lindy's gran and granddad dropped me off, and they waited to make sure I got into the house.

They put their four ancient thumbs up in the air and smiled with triumph and delight – apparently elated that I was able to open the door to my own house – before driving off.

Mum had fallen asleep on the sofa in the blare of the blue TV light, her face flashing like an emergency.

'Mum, I'm home. I have photos,' I whispered.

But she didn't hear me.

I pulled her duvet out of her room and hauled it downstairs, which felt a bit like dragging a large, unenthusiastic pet into the living room. I laid it over her. It was king-sized. It used to be Mum *and* Dad's before Dad met Lindy. It's much too big for one person – and a lot of it drooped and crumpled on the floor beside her. I didn't want her to get cold in the middle of the night.

I went to bed myself, but I couldn't sleep. I twisted myself into a big, agitated knot around my own duvet, and stared for ages at the fake glow-in-the-dark planets and at a damp patch on the ceiling that had been growing and changing over the last few weeks. It had started to look like a squashed-up map of Russia.

Thoughts of Ned wouldn't leave me alone – of him staring off into the distance not seeming to care what anyone said or how anyone felt or what anyone did. And the picture of Ned in my head was always the same – the way he never would talk to anyone, the way he would never talk to me.

I wanted to be like that. I wanted Ned's secrets. I wanted to be cool and careless, just like him.

Moonlight shone through my window as I pulled on my leggings and hoody and left the house. I passed my sleeping mum, tiptoeing to the door, and I headed down to Nettlebog.

12

It was good to be down there in the middle of the night. I breathed in the smells of the place as the moon crept from behind its blue-rimmed cloud. There was a glimmer in the air. I tossed a stone high over the water. It made a splash that spread across the surface in silvery ripples. There was slow lapping and the shiver of that tiny wind in the bushes and there was nothing in particular to do except just be still and think and clear my head a bit.

I mooched around for a while, kicking at twigs and stones underfoot, listening for sounds from the caravan. Watching to see if there were signs of anyone up and about, which at first, there weren't.

But then I heard a noise that sounded exactly like the beginning of thunder – as if something gigantic was tumbling towards me – and the noise got louder as if it was inside my head too. The thick trees looked like dark holes. I wrestled my way behind one of them. My face got scratched and my breath came in loud gulps. My legs trembled as if the ground was moving, which actually it turns out, it was.

It was Ned, riding his horse – both of them glowing in the moonlight. I don't know why but I felt scared then – scared of staying where I was, scared of going home.

The horse ran fast and free and the sound of its hooves *thullumping* around the field felt like a secret code that I couldn't understand, shuddering through me. I kept still, looking out from behind the branches of my hiding tree and I kept seeing a half-smile on Ned's face and the glistening focus in his eyes.

I thought perhaps he saw me too. At least he stared in my direction for approximately ten seconds. And there was that brashness that I'd often seen in his face, but also now there was something else, and it was joy.

In that creamy moonlight moment, it seemed clearer than it had ever been that there were a thousand things about him that I didn't know – that he could go places and do things I couldn't ever imagine. His grip was even and his back was strong and there was an effortlessness about him, the way he stayed firm on the back of that horse who was kicking out a wild dance.

I stayed hunkered down. I pressed my knuckles into the hard earth.

I don't know how long it was before the rumble of the gallop faded and disappeared. The only thing I know is that my feet were numb and my fists were lumps, so clumsy and cold that I couldn't uncurl them. The sun was beginning to come up and a brilliant thing had happened.

Nettlebog had been transformed.

The bushes had exploded in a dazzle of yellow flowers that smelled like popcorn – butter-coloured blankets of bloom, powdery with pollen. The bushes were covered in thousands of pink-pale blossoms as if someone had sneaked in overnight to spray the place with luminous paint and fill it with mini bundles of candyfloss.

Nettlebog Lane was a party of colour. It's ridiculous how lovely it suddenly was.

Mum had eventually woken up. When she couldn't find me, she rang Dad to ask where I was. Dad had pointed out that it was very early the morning after his wedding and Mum had pointed out that she *knew* that, but that *his* daughter, *her* daughter, *their* daughter, wasn't home yet.

When they both stopped arguing and when they faced the fact that I was missing – that's when they went mad. In a way it was nice to think of them doing something together, even if it was only having a collective convulsion of panic. Dad had almost called the police.

When I got back, they'd gone properly mad. I'd been a bit apologetic, but not very.

I hadn't gone far, I'd explained.

'And, what are *you* doing here, Dad? And what are you both freaking out for? Lindy must feel sort of annoyed that you're gone.'

And he'd said, 'Yeah, tell me about it.'

'Some way to start your married life together,' I'd said, and Dad said, 'Minty, honestly, if I wasn't so relieved, I'd strangle you, seriously, I would.'

'That's not very nice,' I said. 'Not very fatherly.'

'You know, Minty, you have to get used to this. Lindy and I are married now and maybe that's not easy for you or your mum, but you're going to have to adjust.'

And I told him I didn't know why he was making such a big deal out of it. I told him that for his information, me and Mum were completely fine and that as a matter of fact he was the only one who was making this massive thing about it.

'Cool your jets, Dad,' I said then. But he didn't laugh. He didn't even smile.

'Look, love, it was only because we were worried,' Mum had said after Dad had left, explaining why they'd gone so psycho.

'How was it, anyway?' she asked.

'It was fabulous, it was incredible, it was like nothing I'd ever seen,' I said.

'Wow. Really?' said Mum.

'Oh,' I said. 'You mean the wedding? Sorry, yeah, the wedding was OK.'

The following Monday, I wondered if the whole thing had maybe been a dream. Ned strutted into school. I glanced at him but he ignored me the same as he always ignored me. The same as he ignored everyone.

'I saw him on Saturday night,' I said to Dougie.

'Who? What?' said Dougie.

'Ned,' I said. 'Ned Buckley.'

'Where?'

'I went down to Nettlebog.'

'Hey, that's the thing the three of us are supposed to do together. I don't like it when you go there without the rest of us.'

'Look, it was late, there was a fire in my head. I kind of felt like being on my own.'

Dougie said if there was a fire in my head then I should have called him and Laura, considering how they were my professional fire-in-the-head-putter-outers.

'Anyway it's not completely surprising you saw Ned there, seeing as that's where he lives.'

'I know, but he was on his horse.'

'Again, not exactly ground-breaking stuff, Mints. Everyone knows about his horses. Haven't we seen him scaring the life out of Mr Doyle on one of them?'

'Yes, but Dougie . . . I mean . . . he's like no one I've ever seen. He leaped like he and that horse were made of air. No one can do the things I saw him do. He's not just a boy who messes around on horses. He's kind of a . . .'

'Kind of a what?'

'A horse genius.'

'I don't know why you're so impressed,' Brendan chipped in, squinting slightly. 'There's a law – and it says that kids riding horses like that on bumpy ground with no supervision – kids even owning horses – is not allowed.'

Brendan's dad worked for the council. He said there'd been loads of problems with mangy old ponies that used to wander onto the road near the Ballyross roundabout.

'This wasn't a mangy old pony. This was his brilliant, sleek, fabulous horse, the same one he rode to school on that day.'

'Yeah, anyway, you need a licence to own a horse and papers and there are checks that have to be done. Oh, yeah, and by the way, I thought Saturday was the night of your Dad's wedding.'

'It was. I went to Nettlebog very late. After I'd got home, long after I was supposed to be in bed.'

'Ooooh, bad girl, Minty,' Brendan teased. 'Did you get into trouble?'

'Yeah, now that you mention it, everyone went mad.'

I didn't see Ned for a couple of days after that, but then at the end of that week there he was, sauntering along beside the lockers.

'I saw you riding a horse.'

It was a stupid conversation opener, I know, but I'd practised a few other lines in my head and they had sounded even stupider.

'Yeah. I take him out at night. He's great in the dark.'

'Ah. Right,' I said. 'That's class.'

He shrugged his shoulders.

'Is that the horse you own?' I asked.

'What business is it of yours?'

'None,' I admitted.

'Then why are you asking me?'

'I didn't mean . . . you see it's just that . . . erm . . . he's beautiful.'

And then he smiled and everything about Ned's face changed and he was looking at me – properly .

'Yes,' he said.

'Dagger,' he said then, after this long pause which he'd spent gazing right into my eyes, and I said, 'What?' and he said, 'Dagger's his name.'

'Good name,' I said.

'The other one's not as fast but she's strong too.'

'Oh, right, yeah, she's beautiful, grey and black-eyed and perfect.'

'How do you know what she's like?'

'Erm . . . I . . . I don't remember. Someone told me.'

I stood and I swung my arms for some reason and then stopped suddenly realising how stupid that must have appeared..

'Do you . . . I mean – do you think? Maybe I could . . .'

Suddenly it felt as if there were rocks in my mouth getting in the way of each other and stopping my words from coming out the way they normally would.

Ned didn't nod his head or ask me what I meant or

71

encourage me to speak more clearly. He just waited.

'Could I come and visit them maybe?' I managed eventually.

'Visit who?' he asked.

'The horses.'

'I dunno. Maybe. If you like,' was his not-particularly-encouraging reply.

I thought it might have been the beginning of an even longer conversation, I mean, I thought we were sort of getting into our stride, but Ned's conversations had a habit of stopping abruptly. He swivelled on his heel and walked off, leaving me watching his back.

'I'm never going to understand him,' I said out loud, before I even realised I'd spoken.

He was impossible to figure out, OK.

And that felt even more true after what Dougie told me.

13

Dougie's parents always get a Chinese takeaway on Saturdays and Dougie'd been sitting in the car waiting for them, which was when he saw my mum standing at the corner talking to Ned. It wasn't just a short chat, either, Dougie said, when I asked him for more details. It was long and lively and it involved a fair amount of laughter on both sides.

'Are you sure it was Ned?' I asked, and Dougie said he was positive.

'OK, so what were they talking about?' I asked.

'Minty, look, I haven't a clue. I was across the road. The windows were shut.'

'What did it *seem* as if they were talking about?' I tried, doing my best to pull more information out of him and feeling confused.

'Minty, honestly, I dunno, but whatever it was, as I said, Ned was laughing. It sort of looked like she was telling him jokes or something. I kept on thinking how odd it was.'

It was odd OK. None of us had ever seen Ned laughing.

'So, how are things, Mum?'

'Things are fine!' she said cheerily as we sat down to dinner. Rice noodles, beans, chickpeas.

'Mum, how do you know Ned Buckley? Dougie saw you talking to him on Main Street yesterday.'

'What?' said Mum, frowning.

'The guy in my class, Ned Buckley, who lives in Nettlebog – you know, where you're always telling me not to go. Dougie saw you talking to him for ages yesterday. On the corner. Ned was laughing?'

'Gosh, Minty, that's puzzling. I don't know what on earth you're talking about.'

'So you weren't on Main Street yesterday? You didn't talk to anyone?'

'No, darling. Dougie must be mistaken.'

You could see Dougie was beginning to regret ever mentioning it. He sighed loudly when I asked him later,

'Are you sure it was my mum?'

'Minty,' he said. 'I know what your mum looks like. I was staring straight at her. It was definitely her.'

I went on about it for so long that in the end Dougie suggested that we should go to Nettlebog and ask Ned about the whole thing himself since he reckoned it was beginning to feel like a mystery and he reckoned I wouldn't have a moment's peace, none of us would, until it was solved.

It was getting dusky by the time we got there. The trees around the caravan were very silent and still and we got a strange feeling as we brushed through them and moved towards the Buckley caravan. We'd been so sure and confident about our strategy. We'd planned to walk straight up to the door and knock, but it was obvious that for some reason, everyone was losing their nerve.

'Look, maybe we shouldn't be hanging around here,' said Laura. 'I think this could probably be called trespassing.'

'Don't be ridiculous, this is a public place, everyone has a right to be here,' I said.

Dougie kept glancing over to the sheds. We could hear gentle shifting coming from that direction, and slowly then, we wandered towards those sounds.

As soon as I saw Ned's horses close up, I realised that this was something I'd been longing for, that it was part of the reason I was down here in the first place, that maybe none of the other reasons mattered quite as much. We patted them, and we stayed for a while and they looked at us with warm friendly eyes until Laura thought she heard another noise.

'What's that?' she whispered, and Dougie and herself stood up, alert and twitchy-looking and they started to seem kind of edgy and paranoid too and then soon they were both saying things like, 'I think we'd better just leave it.'

That's when I saw a light appearing suddenly from behind the trees and I said, 'Listen, go home if you want to, it doesn't bother me, but I came here to find something out, and I'm going to stick around until I do.'

'OK,' they said together, and then Laura and Dougie grabbed their bikes and legged it faster than I'd ever seen them legging it in their lives.

I crept into the thicket and the caravan glowed there in the middle of it. I looked in at the window and I could see Gran poking the stove with one of her sticks, and then Ned appeared, wearing a hoody, bending down to reach something in the kitchen – and then moving to the fire and sipping from a large mug, with his elbows planted on the table.

I was shivering now. I couldn't look away, even though it suddenly felt wrong to be there, watching. I mean, I wasn't watching, or should I say, there wasn't anything to see – except them chatting easily to one another, and Gran was listening to him, and he was paying attention to her too, in a way that made me feel like even more of a stranger to them both. He swiped his hand through his hair.

I thought for a moment about what I might say to him, how I might begin to explain what I was doing there staring in at him and his gran, and I knew I wasn't going to be able to find the words and anything I said wouldn't have sounded like a proper explanation.

And so I did what the others had done. I turned and I ran.

14

After me, Ned was flying through the trees on the back of his horse, galloping faster than I'd ever seen anyone gallop. It looked, for a terrifying second, as though he was going to crash into me. And everything felt like it had slowed down and the horse was very close and somebody was going to die and I was sure it was going to be me.

'What are you doing?' I shouted at him.

'What are *you* doing?' he shouted, him and his horse dancing around me.

'Nothing, I mean, I . . .'

'I'm warning you not to come around and scare my gran or mess with my horses. What kind of person creeps up and stares in at someone's window like that?'

Suddenly, I wasn't just awkward or uncomfortable. Suddenly, I was mortified.

He and his horse breathed fast and fierce and right at that moment I couldn't look him in the eyes, I couldn't even look in his direction.

There was mud and dirt flying everywhere then, and a tufty grassy cloud, as Ned and his horse twisted and leaped. Ned yelled something very loud that I didn't understand. He flipped around. If I hadn't seen him do it, I wouldn't have believed it. He jumped over one of the high Nettlebog bushes and headed off along the riverbank. There was nothing but silence then – that and the ghostly memory of his voice floating in the air.

'I'm sorry, Ned Buckley,' I said to myself.

And I thought of the soft smile he'd given me by the lockers and how his face had been like sunshine and I wondered how this boy here could even be the same person I wanted to get to know.

I kept thinking about how angry I'd made him and I kept trying to imagine what he must have thought when he'd seen me standing, staring in at him. I'd been lurking in the shadows and I wasn't somebody that he'd expected to see. Perhaps he hadn't even known who it was at first, and then when he did know, maybe he thought there was something in my intention that he needed to protect himself from. Maybe he'd been scared of me, I thought for a moment, but then that seemed wrong too.

'We are the ones who are scared of Ned – not the other way around,' I said to myself, thumping myself on the chest, in my room a few nights later. I hadn't been able to think of anything else.

But no matter how outraged I tried to make myself, I realised that the misunderstanding had surely been my fault more than anyone's. I realised too, that I wasn't going to be able to leave things the way they were.

I couldn't allow Ned to think the things he might be thinking about me. Not for another second.

There were truths I needed to find. Truths about Ned – and ones inside myself – that I needed to understand. It felt urgent.

'Muuuum, I'm going for a walk,' I shouted up the stairs, throwing my jacket on.

'Good idea: exercise, fresh air,' shouted Mum, who was in bed on the Internet.

I cycled fast and firm again, and I dashed through the Nettlebog archway, not bending or swerving to avoid the spiky branches that scraped my face and whipped at my legs. I was a straight line of willpower and I marched quickly through the cluster of trees that stood like bodyguards around the Buckley caravan. I didn't wait. I knocked on the door, three times. And I breathed in and out a few times before he opened it.

'I'm sorry.'

Ned lifted an eyebrow.

'You know, coming down here the other night and waiting outside in the dark. I didn't mean to make you angry or give your gran a fright. I think I invaded your territory. I didn't mean to.'

'What did you mean to do then?' he asked, his arms above his head, holding on to the frame of the door.

'Look, that's why I'm here. I just want to explain.'

'Explain what?'

'What I actually was doing. I came down here to ask you a question. I know you've met my mum. Dougie saw you talking to her on Main Street. Why would you do that? How do you even know her? There's something going on that I don't understand and I guess what I want is for you to tell me what that is.'

'What it is,' he said, exhaling loudly and looking over my shoulder at something else, 'is none of your business.'

'Ha! So there *is* something you're not telling me! There's no point denying it. It makes you look dead suspicious. You should tell me what's going on.'

'I'm not going to do that.'

'Why not?'

'For one thing, I'm not obliged to tell anyone anything. And for another thing, if I did, it would only make things worse.'

'How would it?'

'Trust me, I know what I'm talking about.'

'What do you mean? You're not doing yourself any favours. Seriously, Ned. Like, I get that you're annoyed with me for creeping around down here, I understand. But don't you see? This is important to me.

'I have a reliable eyewitness who has seen you talking to my mum. And you and my mum are both denying it

81

and I get this feeling that someone is trying to drive me crazy. And what I'm asking is for you to explain it to me because I don't understand.'

'Why are you so interested?' he asked, looking past me and then straight into my eyes again in a way that made me feel nervous.

'Look, OK,' I said. 'Maybe it's none of my business, it's just that – you see, my mum hasn't done a proper smile or a proper laugh for a long time, and Dougie said she and you were having a happy-looking conversation and in my head, Ned, I was like, "What are the most silent boy in my class and my mum doing, talking to each other like that, when it's been ages since she had that kind of a conversation with her own daughter?"

'It doesn't make sense to me. You never talk to anyone. My mum might be full of fake smiley-ness and pretend good news, but she hasn't laughed for months, not the way Dougie said she was laughing when she was talking to you. So, the thing is, Ned, I'm just puzzled. Her on the corner and you there with her, and the two of you acting like you're both the most entertaining humans ever.'

That was it, and I only realised it when I started to talk to him. For some reason, *he'd* managed to find the best things in my mum, and bring them out and I began to realise what my problem was: I was jealous.

'I just want to know what's going on. But she's not telling me and I guess you're not going to tell me either.'

I'd been so busy trying to explain what I meant – even though I wasn't that sure myself – that I hadn't noticed myself getting so loud and shrill. I realised then, though, that I was practically screeching. Ned held his hand horizontally in front of my face and lowered it like it was a lift – his signal, I guessed, for getting me to shut up.

'Right, OK, Minty, thanks, and now if you'll just calm the hell down, I'll tell you. I will. OK?'

I was already sorry for raising my voice and getting so hyper, but not nearly as sorry as I was going to feel in a minute.

Suddenly Ned looked sort of sad. He didn't do any background explaining or any preparing. He just came right out with it:

'I can't read,' he said. 'I don't want anyone to know.'

15

Ned had been getting reading lessons from my mum. On Saturday mornings. He'd got her to promise not to say a word to anyone about it, especially after he'd found out she was my mum.

It turns out there were lots of things I'd never have imagined or predicted about Ned. Mainly about how he was just as uncertain and insecure as anyone else. How coming to school wasn't a boring snore of a thing like he acted it was. Coming to school was an ordeal for him. He told me about how much bravery it took every day and how hard it kept being, to pretend he had the slightest clue about what was going on.

He'd never have known about the reading and writing lessons in the library if it hadn't been for Serena, who had spotted he'd been having difficulty with some of the basics. She was the one who found out about the free support that was available – none of the other teachers knew anything about the Mountain of Knowledge.

'Is that what the place is called?' I asked him, and he

said yes, there was a nice sign above the door with those words and some good artwork.

He told me that Serena had taken it on herself to drive down to Nettlebog in her red Cinquecento. She was the one who'd suggested to his gran that he'd be the perfect person to get some extra help in the library. And my mum had offered to be his literacy tutor and he'd agreed to that – but only on condition that she promised to keep quiet about it.

It's hard to pretend you don't know someone when you do, or I should say it's easy to forget to pretend when you happen to bump into them at unexpected times, and both Mum and Ned forgot that day on the corner of Main Street.

'When I met her, it felt natural to chat. We get on. We were planning the next session. She tried to keep it secret when you asked, because she didn't want to break her promise to me.'

I was impressed and kind of annoyed.

'She's not usually that good at keeping promises,' I pointed out.

'I don't want anyone to know how thick I am,' he said. 'I'm a bit afraid.'

'Ned Buckley, afraid? Seriously?' I said.

'What did you think?'

'We thought you hated us.'

'Why did you think that?'

'Because you didn't want to be friends, not even when we offered. Because of the day when you wouldn't shake Laura's hand.'

Ned had a policy – which involved not shaking hands with anyone he didn't know yet.

'It's often happened,' he explained, 'that you risk shaking hands with someone whose hand you find out afterwards you've no interest in shaking.'

'Yeah, see, that's why we thought you didn't care about anything to do with school or with us. There isn't a single person in our class who'd have thought you were frightened of anything. Everyone's afraid of *you*.'

Ned smiled then and he said, 'That's the way I'd like to keep it, if you don't mind.'

His secrets were safe with me, I told him.

He said the first moment he'd realised that it had been me standing outside that time in the dark, he'd thought I'd come to see the horses, like I'd said I wanted to.

He'd have been delighted to see me in that case, but then he said my eyes had been wide and weird-looking. And when I'd just turned around and sprinted off, that was when he began to wonder what I was up to. I told him I wasn't up to anything. The whole thing had been a misunderstanding. I was glad we were sorting it out.

We ended up talking about what Ned had said to Brendan the first day Ned had opened his mouth – about how he acted aloof and cool and how the reason he'd done that, he explained, was to hide. It was a cover up, he said, for the things he felt unable – for the things he couldn't do.

'What was the deal with the galloping episode in school that terrorised Mr Doyle?'

'I wasn't trying to frighten anyone,' he replied.

'Then what were you trying to do?'

He said he wasn't sure, except that it had to do with feeling so different.

He said he reckoned that if the others saw him riding on Dagger, brave and fast like he did that day, then they might realise that he was full of skill. They might see what he could do, and if everyone saw that then he mightn't feel so bad about not being able to read.

'I guess I was just trying to impress.'

'Bad strategy,' I said.

And that's when Ned smiled and when he smiled, my fingers went numb.

'You're right, I guess. Pretty stupid, OK, when you put it like that.'

And his smile grew wide and gorgeous with his teeth showing. And I don't know why I should have been so surprised, but Ned had great teeth. The smile made him look wonderful and then it turned into a laugh and I think he was laughing at himself a bit and soon I was laughing too – at Ned's logic, at the memory of Mr Doyle's shocked face and of everyone in the class standing in the yard frozen, eyes like flashlights.

Tears fell down my face and off my chin and we

laughed for so long that we nearly forgot what we we'd been laughing at.

Laughter can feel like an enormous thing sometimes, big and important, like freedom or courage. And for us that day, laughing was like a doorway to a new place that I was able to walk into and it was such a simple thing that I wondered why it had felt so impossible before.

Gran had appeared just behind him with the same kindness in her eyes.

'This is my gran,' said Ned, 'And, Gran, this is Minty.'

Gran said, 'Sure I know who it is. Minty and I are old friends, aren't we, lovey?' She said it was nice to see me again, that there was no need to go creeping round the place, that I was welcome any time.

'Now the two of you need to decide whether to come in or go out. That draught would cut you in two.'

Inside the caravan were patchwork blankets everywhere, folded in piles. Low lamps shone uneven light and threw ragged shadows on the walls. And even though it was small and you had to bend down to get through the door, there was something about the spaces in there that made it possible to breathe steadily and think comfortable thoughts. Tins and boxes and shelves and chests and drawers and colour and blankets and light so cosy and everything condensed and bunched together.

Flames were dancing in a black stove, and there were

two soft chairs facing each other and everything felt warm and happy. The kitchen was just a counter with a little grill and four knobbly loaves of bread lined up beside the hob. Frying pans dangled from a hook in the ceiling, and they swung back and forth every time Ned or his gran opened or closed a door.

Covering the walls, tacked with drawing pins, were photos. Hundreds of pictures of Dagger and Phoebe and of riders and horses that I did not know.

There was an old photo of Ned on the wall but when I looked more closely, it wasn't Ned. Same face OK, different eyes. A boy's face: muddy and grinning, holding a silver cup above his head. And there was another picture of the same boy, this time on a horse, leaning forward. His arms were around the horse's neck and he had that same grin and it was so like Ned it was confusing.

'I thought that was you for a second,' I said, worrying that it might be rude, staring at photos like that without saying anything.

'That's my da,' he said. 'Everyone says I'm the image of him.' And when he said that, there was a dip of sadness in his voice.

As soon as Dagger saw Ned, he whickered and nodded his head as if he was getting ready for something great. Phoebe was even more beautiful than I remembered. I patted her on the nose and she pressed her face against mine and I must have tickled the top of her head because for a second her whole body shuddered, and it made me jump, and Ned laughed again.

'Once you've been kind to a horse, they'll never forget you,' Ned told me. She likes you now, I can see it. It's clear, and she trusts you, and you see the sort of horse she is, if she trusts you, from now on she always will.

Ned told me that horses were loyal and fierce and they were gentle and strong and he wished that human beings were more like horses, because if they were, the future of the world would be secure.

And I could feel the warmth of the horses' bodies and see the spark of connection in their eyes, and it wasn't hard to understand what he meant.

Gran was just like any regular grandparent. I mean she did things I imagine every grandparent does, not that I'd know, as the only grandparents I have live in Florida and I can't remember what they even look like. Anyway, what I mean is that she made cakes and sandwiches and seemed almost constantly worried about whether we were hungry.

I asked for a go on the swing and Ned said of course.

'It's good fun, for a homemade jacked-up kind of a thing.'

'Is there room for another person up there?' he asked, and I said, 'It's your swing, you should know.'

In a single leap he was sitting beside me. The curve of the tyre squashed us together. We couldn't help it.

The Nettlebog caravan is one of those important places in the world where you can say what you think and be who you are.

I loved the feeling that it gave me and the things it made me say. But what I loved most about it was learning about the real Ned, the Ned who was going to be my friend after all.

'I don't get it – Ned Buckley? The guy who never talks to anyone? The guy who spends his life being unfriendly and cold and too good for us? Your new best friend?'

'Hey, calm down. You should all give him the benefit of the doubt, like I'm trying to.'

'Why is everyone acting so snotty?' I asked Brendan. 'You are being so unfair to him.'

'I'm not that sure Ned Buckley deserves your friendship,' Dougie reckoned.

'Yeah, well, I'm not sure that's any of your business,' I replied.

16

After that visit, calling on Ned and Gran became a part of my life, and they got so used to seeing me that they'd start to wonder where I was on the days I didn't show up. Gran had made plans to visit her sister in Kerry, and she was thrilled to know that she was going to be able to leave Ned without worrying that he was going to be completely on his own.

'It's a comfort to know you're about the place,' was how she put it.

Whenever I called in, I got in the habit of bringing my books. And I said to Ned something like, look, we might as well do it together and he said fair enough or maybe he said yeah, OK, but anyway, we began reading stuff at the same time, and I'd call out some words and he'd call out others and sometimes I'd pretend to get a word wrong and eventually I noticed he started to correct me. He must have been getting on superbly with Mum because even I could see that he was improving a lot.

Afterwards, Ned and I would head out to the horses,

and Gran would make sure that we always took a flask of tea, to keep us going, she said.

I asked him if he or his gran thought there might be something magic about Nettlebog and he said no but I could be forgiven for thinking it. Wherever there are happy, well-cared-for horses, a place was always going to feel special. They were the ones that *made* the magic, Ned said. Dagger was beautiful and everything, but Phoebe – soon, it was as if she belonged to me. That's what it felt like anyway.

'You should have a go on her,' Ned said.

'Oh no. I'd be afraid.'

'What would you be afraid of?'

'She might go too fast. I could fall.'

Gran said there wasn't much use in doing something unless you were a bit frightened but she said that being scared of falling was the same thing as being scared of living and that it would be more in my line to get that fear out of my system as soon as I could and a good way to start would be to learn to ride Phoebe.

'Anyway, I'll have your back,' Ned said. 'Everything's going to be fine.'

'Relax,' Phoebe's even breathing seemed to say, 'You are safe,' was the message in her whinny. And I whispered back into her ear and Phoebe began to trot and it didn't feel too scary at all.

The horses would go anywhere he told them, and that day we trotted for miles along the water's edge, way, way beyond the caravan till we were far past the other side of town and in places I'd never seen before.

Ned told me that every horse has its own way of moving, and when you get to know them, you can tell the difference between them even if you are blindfolded.

Phoebe was light and sharp and precise and there was a grace about her that's difficult to explain if you haven't seen her.

Some people could practise on the back of a horse for a hundred years and still not understand how to ride. Others can get the sense of a horse just once, and it wakes up the gift inside them. That's what Ned and his gran said I had: a gift inside me that was waiting to get out. I desperately wanted to be as good as Ned and I would have tried for ever, but they said it wasn't practice that separated the horse people from the non-horse people. It was something else that couldn't be named or defined. Something that I was able to prove, not just to them but to myself. I was able to ride Phoebe, and I knew how she turned and what she responded to, and I learned about her bravery and how to bring it to the surface and according to Gran, I was a horse person – a born rider. And maybe it took longer than I remember, but it feels like it was no time before I was jumping after Ned, over bushes and between the great trees of Nettlebog and soon I was trampling along the bank as if someone was chasing us, and soon there was this thing between me and Phoebe that no one was going to be able to break. Like a chain, only invisible, and light and magic.

You don't remember learning things. It's just that one day comes and you can do something so well that you can't imagine a time when you once couldn't do it.

I loved it when we rode, but I loved it too when our rides were over and when we went back to the caravan for tea, our faces were always pink and we were always in great form and Gran said we looked beautiful. That's the exact word she used.

The air makes you beautiful when you gallop through it. That's what it felt like on Phoebe. As if the air had kissed my cheeks and brushed my hair.

Phoebe could leap over the prickly hedgerows nearly as well as Dagger – and there were long lanes that connected a hundred back gardens in Ballyross where Ned said I could learn to go fast. The kids who were playing in their gardens would stand looking at us with their mouths open and their arms hanging as we went tearing past. And sometimes I'd make the loud whooping noise that I'd learned from Ned. I don't know why. I hate drawing attention to myself usually. But when you're galloping on the back of a horse you love, you want the world to see you and you can't help shouting. I don't think you can avoid it.

Gran was leaving for her trip to Kerry to see her sister. She was going to be gone for five days, and exactly as she'd predicted, Ned didn't want to go with her. It was just as well, she'd said, because she didn't want him to miss any more school.

I'd promised I'd look in on him and keep an eye on him and make sure he didn't get lonely, and just be about the place while she was gone.

I told her that there was nothing I'd prefer more than being about the place in Nettlebog. She said I was a good neighbour. She said they were lucky to know me and I told her the feeling was mutual.

'Let's go to school together tomorrow,' Ned suggested. I said that was a great idea and it was obvious Gran was thrilled. And I could feel something in my heart lifting, because it had started to fill up a bit with a mixture of things. Things like loyalty and connection and hope and friendship.

17

Next morning sun seeped through my window and I was up before my alarm rang. I had a fistful of muesli and a glass of milk and I skidded out of the door. Mum had only just made it out of bed.

'Have you had breakfast, Minty?' she yelled after me. I waved to her from my bike and she stuck her head out of the window and said,

'Minty, that's not the way to school!'

'Don't worry,' I shouted back. 'I'm collecting someone.'

Ned came out munching an apple.

'Morning!' He smiled. 'Follow me.'

He tramped across the scrubby ground towards the horse shed.

'Where are you going? We'll be late .'

'Come on,' he replied. 'I've to go and say hello to Dagger and Phoebe.'

I could have said no, but I didn't.

He gave me an apple for Phoebe and he fed one to Dagger, who nuzzled him. I patted Phoebe, who seemed fidgety. I didn't know why.

Ned opened the door and led Dagger out.

'OK, what are you doing now?' I asked.

'What does it look like I'm doing?' he said, as Phoebe stepped out with her dainty feet into the sunshine too, and shook her whole body as if she was getting ready.

'I don't know.'

And he said, 'I'm trying to give you something'

'Give me something?'

'Yes.'

'What?'

'A story to tell.'

'A story?' I said, scrunching up my eyes to see him better in the hard morning light.

'Yes.'

He was steadying both the horses now and lining them up beside each other.

'Everyone needs a good story. And, OK, you have a few more to tell now that you're . . . you know . . . a horse person, but you see, I keep getting this feeling you don't have a properly good one yet.'

The horses were head-butting me gently, as if they were trying to persuade me the same way Ned was.

'I've plenty of stories, thanks very much,'

'You don't have this one.'

'Which one is that?'

'The story about the day you rode to school on a horse with Ned Buckley.'

'Ned, has anyone told you you're mad?'

'Yes,' he said and his grin made my heart flip over and it made me think for a second that I could be a bit more like him, a bit more adventurous and that I could do things that most people can't dream of doing.

I swung my bag on my back and I jumped up on Phoebe.

Before we got going, I glanced up at Dougie's house and I saw him standing at his kitchen window. He was holding a cup of tea but it looked as if it was suspended in mid-air. His mouth was wide open. I waved. He kept on looking at me but he didn't wave back, and to be honest, I didn't have time to wonder why. I didn't even care that much.

I was too busy making a story with Ned Buckley.

That day, Phoebe and I had to gallop faster than we ever had so we could keep up with Ned and Dagger. On past the Ballyross roundabout and past the rows of houses. I could feel the wind in my face and Phoebe's warmth and her strength.

'Hold on!' Ned shouted, as if every atom of me wasn't holding on already.

So that was the day Ned and I raced along the back

lanes to school. The wind was pressing our clothes against our bodies and I could hear the horses' steady breathing and the exact same rhythm of their gallop, and I was proud of myself. Ned was laughing and I looked over at the way he crouched when riding his horse, at his grip on Dagger's mane, at the focus in his eyes. And I tried my best to do the same.

'How did you learn to do this?' I shouted over at him, still barely keeping up.

'I've been in training since I was four,' he shouted back.

'You're getting ready for the Ballyross Race, aren't you?'

'Yeah, I am. That's exactly what I'm doing. How did you know?'

'I know plenty of things,' I replied.

The bareback rule of the Ballyross Race suited Ned perfectly. You'd never have got a saddle on Dagger, I reckon, no matter how hard you tried.

Ned made me promise to keep any news about the race to myself.

'Of course I won't tell anyone,' I said. He said it might seem obvious to me now, but if there was any pressure put on me for any reason to let a single person know that he was planning to race, then I might feel differently. No matter how anyone might try to get information out of me, I was to be as silent as a stone.

'OK, OK, I get it. My lips are totally sealed,' I said. And

he'd said good because the one thing we don't want to do is give the rest of them any advance warning. We want to take everyone by surprise. Taking by surprise is part of the game.

Serena was standing at the school gates shading her eyes, watching us. It was too far away to see her face, but already I'd imagined she was furious. Too late to do anything about that, I thought. As we galloped along the last stretch, you could see others gathering at the gates too.

'Let's give them something to look at,' Ned suggested. 'Come on, three times around the yard, see what you're made of.'

It was wrong and we were going to be in trouble but I didn't care. Besides, the horses were just getting into their stride and I felt reckless and bold, and so we did. We raced around like lunatics. By then the whole class was watching, and some of them were even cheering us on.

A man had turned up and as soon as Ned saw him, the happiness in his face disappeared. The man was from the council, Ned said. Ned and his gran had met him a good few times before.

'Here,' said Ned, 'I'm going to take them home. If anyone asks you, tell them it was my fault I led you astray.'

It turns out that the man was Brendan's dad. His shoulders were exactly the same shape. He and his son cast the same shadow.

Mr Kirby marched up to our classroom and by the time I arrived he was in there shouting at Serena. As soon as I came in, he turned his attention to me.

'Where is the boy? The boy you were with?'

'Gone home,' I said.

'Ha, you see! He's just scarpered,' said Mr Kirby.

'He is a hooligan.'

'I know of the things he does too. He gathers other hooligans around him and they race down by the old factory. I've heard them screaming and bellowing on top of their filthy-looking horses.'

Brendan's dad acted as if he was the owner of all the facts and details in the whole world.

'I want you to know that that boy is engaged in a range of illegal unlicensed activity. He is from an unsuitable family. He's a terrible influence and I have told my son that from now on, he is to stay away from him.'

I could have told him there was nothing to worry about there, seeing as Ned never had any interest whatsoever in being anywhere near Brendan.

'The boy is nothing but trouble. A scumbag. Something has to be done about him.'

Serena hadn't interrupted him. She hadn't said a word, but you could see she was getting ready to speak. She leaned forward with her hands flat on the desk.

'I have to say, I am very shocked indeed,' she said, and I had the feeling this was going to be the beginning of a long lecture.

18

A strand had come loose from Serena's tied back hair. '. . . Are you happy?' Mr Kirby said, stabbing his finger in my general direction. 'Your teacher is shocked. Shocked by the things she has seen you and that boy getting up to.'

Serena held up her hand and her pale blue nails spread out like a formation of tiny birds.

She spoke slowly in a quiet voice that everyone was listening to.

'What I am shocked about, Mr Kirby, is that I have been teaching these students for over a year, and until today, I did not know we had such magnificent horse riders in our midst,' she said.

Mr Kirby's features contorted into a frown.

'And what I am also shocked about,' she continued, 'is that many in this town – prominent role models like you, seem to think it is acceptable to refer to a boy, a perfectly good boy, in the way that you have just done.'

'A perfectly good boy?'

'Honestly, Mr Kirby, you must not shout at me in my own classroom.'

He was about to speak again, but Serena raised her hand, and like magic, it silenced him.

'If you think bad things about a boy, and if you spread bad opinions about him, then you should expect him to do things you do not like.'

Brendan's dad pressed his lips together till they went white, and he curled his fingers into fists and stood at the door trying to make himself look big.

'Racing horses in public places is ancient and noble.'

'In the name of sanity,' he said. 'What are you talking about?'

'Mr Kirby,' she said. 'Do you know the difference between a hero and a delinquent? Do you know the difference between recklessness and bravery? Between breaking the law and being a role model for discipline and valour?'

Mr Kirby opened and closed his mouth and his eyes kept staring at her and not blinking. He reminded me of a giant fish.

'Of course you do. The difference is context. Take a muddy field in Dublin and change it to a cobbled square in Siena, and then you will see what I mean.'

'Ned and Minty have skills that honour an ancient tradition. They do what must be done in life. They take the raw, chaotic energy of living and they make it brave and strong.'

'Are you telling me that you *approve* of the havoc he has

caused by riding his horse in random ways, by terrorising this school's teachers and students, by getting one of his classmates involved? You're not seriously going to tell me you think this conduct is acceptable?'

'Mr Kirby, I admit that he can appear to be a little wild. But it seems that you do not fully understand what it takes to be able to do the things that this boy can do.'

Brendan's dad looked like he still had loads more things to say but you could see that Serena was in charge now.

'You have told me very many things this morning – about your thoughts and your feelings on the subject of Ned Buckley, and now *I* am going to tell you some things about him.'

Serena took an enormous breath and sighed.

'If that boy . . .' She pointed towards the door as if Ned might be standing behind it. The red jewels on her bracelet clinked together like bells, and her slim finger stayed steady in the air as she spoke, '. . . If that boy lived in Siena – the town where I come from – everyone would *worship* him.'

She was quiet for a while then.

'The skill, my goodness, the skill,' she whispered eventually. 'It's quite unbelievable. What a boy, what a capacity.

'. . . There would be crowds following him with the palms of their hands held up to the sky as if he were a god. There'd be representatives from every single one of the neighbourhoods, pleading with him . . . begging him to come to train with them and to ride for them.'

A new hush seemed to fall in the room and everything was quiet, except for the sound of Mr Kirby's breath coming out in massive angry puffs.

'I'm glad to say that Ned is likely to be impervious to the insults of grown-ups like you – those who sit in judgement of him even though they know nothing about him.'

Mr Kirby's face was suddenly a weird bluish-red.

'What are you saying to me, Miss Serralunga? What are you trying to tell me here?'

'I am trying to tell you that that boy,' she replied, her voice rising like a melody. 'That boy could be a Palio jockey. He is certainly good enough, absolutely talented enough, definitely brave enough.'

Nobody said anything.

'Now, please get out of my classroom.'

Mr Kirby puffed and clicked and huffed for another while, but then he backed away slamming the door.

'Minty, out here, please,' she said and I got up from my desk and joined her in the hallway.

'Where is Ned?' she asked. I told her he'd gone back home with the horses, that he was worried about what Mr Kirby might do, so he'd decided to take them out of the equation.

'OK, good,' she said.

She asked me where he kept the horses and if they had enough to drink and so on, and I said,

'You're talking about Ned Buckley here. He takes perfect care of those horses. He's a horse expert. The horses are looked after and safe and when it comes to those two animals, nobody has anything to worry about.'

'Right,' Serena said when everyone had settled down again. 'There's been a lot of agitation this morning, and I'm not going to go on about it. But I was not exaggerating. What I said about Ned was true. I meant every word. If he lived in Siena, they'd be getting him ready for the Palio.'

Orla had her hand up.

'Yes, Orla, what is it?'

'Miss, where *is* Siena?'

'And what is the Palio?' said Dougie.

Serena had begun writing her lesson plan on the whiteboard. She stopped, and turned to face us.

'Will someone please tell Orla and Dougie the answer to those questions?'

Nobody said a word.

'What is this?' she asked looking around the room now as if some horrible fact was beginning to dawn on her.

'Gracious me, how am I to understand this silence? Why is it,' she asked, twirling around in full circles now, with her arms spread out, 'that you do not gasp with joy and pride at the sound of those words, the way every civilised human should?'

'*Il Palio*? *Il Palio*?' she repeated.

No one had a clue what she was on about.

'I am filled with calamitous outrage!' she declared, and the bang of her elegant shoe echoed around the room.

'Do those blank faces tell me something I simply cannot believe? Is there not one of you who knows what I'm talking about? *Il Palio*?'

'*La Piazza del Campo*?' she added, looking for some flicker of recognition in our eyes.

'*Le Contrade di Siena*?'

'*Gli Fantini*?'

'Anyone? Anyone? Oh, for goodness' sake!'

More silence.

'Does none of you know what I am talking about? What is *Il Palio*?' said Serena and her words were a slow string of astonishment. '*What is Il Palio*?'

There was only one thing for it. She was going to have to find time to teach us.

19

'There is a square in Italy – a square that's not a square. A square that is the shape of a fan. Siena is the town and the square is the Piazza del Campo.'

It looked as if there was a new and different light shining on Serena's face, even though it was actually quite cloudy and dull outside.

'The sunrise is a spectacular explosion. It throws pink light everywhere. Every day brings a burst of new beginning.

'Waiters whistle as they open their doors and the piazza fills up. Children run, companions chat, tourists sit on the smooth cobbles, gripped with a strange urge to throw away their maps.'

'Why do they want to throw away their maps, Miss?' asked Laura.

'What use do you have for a map if you never want to leave somewhere?' she replied.

Serena began walking around the classroom, brushing past the sides of the bookshelves, her long cardigan floating out behind her, almost catching on one of the hooks by the door. She opened a window and let in the chilly threads of outside.

'In the heat of the afternoon,' she continued, 'the shadow of the clock tower strokes the stone below. Many amble towards its shade like cats.'

'It sounds lovely,' said Laura.

'It is! It is both lovely and it is more than lovely, different from lovely, for it is not a simple, straightforward place, as peaceful and fine as it may feel on such evenings.'

Serena's hands fanned out again – a dreamy kind of echo of the place she was trying to describe.

'It's mystical and strange. The citizens of Siena know how lucky they are to have this place at the heart of their city. The Piazza del Campo is a place that honours togetherness and friendship, a place that's good-natured and sheltered, full of warmth and shade.'

Even Brendan sat forward, leaning his chest on his desk as if he wanted to keep listening.

'And so now, every one of you should have the image of a perfect Piazza del Campo – I want you to let it settle in your mind's eye. Think of the shape of the stone. Think of the pink light that fills it in the mornings and of the peaceful feeling that floats there. Keep that image in your heads, and now let me draw your attention to something else: the thing that happens there twice a year, the thing that changes it utterly: the thing that turns that very same Piazza del Campo into a stage on which the world's most extraordinary drama is played out.'

111

Everyone looked a little bit hypnotised.

'The Piazza del Campo becomes the theatre in which a most ancient race is run. A horse race. Many will tell you that it is the greatest, most terrifying race in the entire world.

'Ninety seconds long – bareback, cut-throat, break-neck – it begins with gunfire and the screaming of the crowd. Ten wild-eyed jockeys ride at a slanted gallop around the Piazza's boundary – risking everything for the banner of victory known as *Il Palio*.'

Her voice was velvet and steel. We stayed absolutely silent.

'When it's over, spectators fall to their knees; some in triumph, some in anguish. Outsiders often ask about the purpose of this frantic ritual, and the passions that it unlocks. The Palio serves many functions, they are told, but mostly it is a reminder of deep and ancient truths: that great changes happen in the blink of an eye; that a peaceful place can be filled with danger; that friends can become enemies; that things are not always as they seem.

'Ned Buckley is not what he appears to be. He is not what he seems. He is not what they say he is. It takes a lot of practice to ride a horse the way he does. Oh, and, Minty, don't misinterpret, you are capable and impressive too. It's just that Ned . . .'

'Yeah, OK, thanks, I get it,' I said. At least she gave me a mention, but it was totally obvious that Ned was the one who had properly astonished her.

The door creaked open. If he'd been trying to slip in unnoticed, that definitely wasn't going to work.

Everyone turned to look at him, Ned Buckley, with the terrible reputation, who everyone was scared of already, who nobody quite knew what to make of. And I got this feeling in the back of my throat that this was one of those crucial moments, where public opinion could swing in some violent direction or another. It was my responsibility. This was my chance to stand up for him and when you have a chance, you must take it, even if you're not a hundred per cent sure how exactly it's going to turn out.

I stood up and I pointed at Ned.

'He's the dark horse,' I announced, but you could see immediately that no one had the slightest clue what I was on about.

'The dark horse of the competition! The Ballyross Race. He could win it. It's famous. It's on next Sunday. And he's going to race in it against some of the toughest riders in the country!'

Ned didn't look proud or embarrassed or anything that I would have expected him to look. He looked cross. He was making the sign of someone having their throat cut and it took me a few more seconds before I realised what I had done – before I understood that he was trying to shut me up.

'There's no race next Sunday. It's been called off. Minty here has the wrong end of the stick altogether.'

Of course Ned had been lying. He was only pretending

the race was cancelled to throw everyone off the scent. The Ballyross Race would never be cancelled. It was an old ritual and there were still a lot of people who would never let a ritual like that die.

'I'm sorry, I feel like an idiot for telling everyone our secret,' I told him later on, when it was just to two of us again.

'Don't worry about it. No harm done,' he replied but still this was one of the times when being with Ned made me feel like a foolish little kid.

We had to find out everything there was to know about the Palio. Serena told us that we had an official project to do. But even if she hadn't, everyone would have gone straight home and looked it up.

The Palio has been happening twice every summer since 1356. It is the greatest horse race in the world.

The ten jockeys are heroes and everybody wants to be one of them, but hardly anybody is. The horses are sturdy and handsome and full of their own reasons for wanting to run faster than anyone else. For the horses, it's nothing to do with honour or glory or money or fame or anything like that. It's to do with doing what they're meant to do, what they're born to do. For them it's not about being loyal to the race. It's about being loyal to the moment.

A crowd, loud and colourful and crammed together, teems in the middle of the square that's like a giant fan. And everything is noisy and the throng is shouting and you can't imagine that the noise is ever going to quieten, but then, in a magic moment, all heads look towards one man who stands at the centre by the starting line: white shirt, solemn face.

The man is holding a gun in the air. Every rider has an expression that is impossible to explain, except to say that it is fearless and frightened at the same time.

In the depths of the loaded silence the gun fires and the crowd lifts like a single thing, and the horses and riders are off – and it seems as if, instead of humans on their backs, there are wings.

Each rider wears a special colour and a hat that represents one of the Sienese neighbourhoods. Each is known as a contrada, which has its own crest and everyone wants their contrada to win.

The race is short and fast, but it's as if those few seconds are the only things in the world.

When the winner crosses the line, grown men cry and hug and kiss and some of them look like they're going to pass out. Thousands of fists punch the air. Thousands of knees hit the ground. Thousands of arms reach towards the sky.

Ned and I had been paired off for the Palio project. Those are some of the things we found out. Ned's reading was much better by then. He stumbled over a word or two every so often, but no more than anyone else. You'd never have known that he'd only just learned.

∨∼

Considering we had known nothing about this place and this race, we managed to find out a massive amount. It wasn't that hard. The Internet is covered in it, if you bother to look.

'It's like going to the moon,' says one of Siena's jockeys in an interview that's on this Italian horse-riding blog we found. *'You can never be the same after you've been a Palio rider. Once you've been part of the Palio the things of the day-to-day are blessed with bravery and courage.'*

∨∼

'Ah, *fantastico*!' Serena had said after Ned and I presented our project, and after everyone had clapped.

And she gazed out of the window and off past the low hills behind our school, and you could see that for a little while she wasn't in Ballyross Secondary any more in front of the lot of us. She was in the Piazza del Campo, part of the feverish crowd.

∨∼

Even Brendan had been interested at first, but he said the

project was taking ages and it was distracting us from the other things we were supposed to be learning.

'Miss, can you remind us why have we been spending this whole week learning about the Palio?'

'Oh, shut up, Brendan,' everyone said, but we should have known by then that it was difficult to keep Brendan quiet.

'My dad says nothing like that is on the curriculum. It doesn't make sense to be devoting this many hours to something as irrelevant as that. We can't ignore reality, and the reality is that there's loads of other stuff we're supposed to be getting on with.'

Serena stared at Brendan for a full ten seconds without saying a word.

'No point in ignoring reality? Why, don't be ridiculous, Brendan, of course there is!' she replied.

'How could anyone dream,' she asked, 'of turning their back on human potential by dealing in the banalities of reality?'

She acted as though she was talking about everyone, but it was perfectly obvious to me that the only person she was talking about was Ned.

'You should come and see the race on Sunday, Miss,' Ned said when everyone was packing up for the day.

'The race?'

'Yes, the Ballyross.'

'But we thought it was called off?' everyone said, more or less in unison.

'Of course it isn't called off.' He smiled. 'But it's better that not everyone knows that.' Ned looked over at Brendan who was sitting with his legs spread out and his arms folded. 'Isn't that right, Brendan?' he said.

'I know plenty of guys like Brendan,' Ned claimed later, when we were brushing the horses in the dark. 'He's the kind of guy who'll talk turkey when it comes to striking a deal, when it comes to keeping his mouth shut. Everybody has their price, and he's cheaper than most.'

Ned had paid Brendan not to tell his father that the Ballyross Race was on. Brendan was going to keep his mouth shut about it. Ned was sure of it.

20

I don't know how human instincts work. It's a mystery, I guess. I was coming home from school that day, half-jogging down our street, in a hurry to tell Mum about our project and the top marks we'd got for it – with an idea in my head that later I might go down to Ned's – when I knew something was different, something was wrong. First it was a motionlessness in the air – a feeling that was not the same as the usual afternoon calmness on our road on a weekday afternoon. A bitter wind began to blow and a coldness washed over me as if an icy rain had begun to fall.

I put my key in the door, but when I tried to push it open, there was something on the other side stopping me.

'What the . . .'

I whispered Mum's name, then I said it louder and then I shouted it.

'Mum. Mum. Mum.'

And I was hoping to hear her reply, 'What Minty?' or 'Calm down, I'm right here,' or even 'Goodness me, Minty, what are you shouting for?'

But there were none of those sounds. Instead there was just a faint moan. A weight was on the other side of the door and that weight was Mum.

'Mum, Mum?'

'Minty, love,' came her voice like a thin thread.

'I've fallen. I'm here in the hall and I can't move. I've tried. There's something wrong with my leg.'

And after that I heard another moan and Mum stopped talking so I hadn't a clue what to do.

I knocked on every door on our street. Nobody was home and then I ran up and down the road at least three times when I should have been ringing an ambulance or doing something practical to get help, but my brain wasn't working properly.

I couldn't get Dad on his phone. And I couldn't think of anyone else to ring so I rang Ned.

'Ned, I need you to get your gran to drive her van here right now, please. It's an emergency. It's serious. I need your help.'

I knew by then that Ned's gran has that reliable solid thing that some people have which makes you know you can count on them. So, I sat waiting for her on our front step with my elbows on my knees breathing fast and talking to Mum with our front door between us. Even though Mum had stopped talking to me.

It came quickly – a great roar and a clattery rattle burst through the air and I saw it bumping along down our road with clouds of smoke belching out of the back of it. Gran's Nettlebog van. Dirty and rusty and white. It stopped very suddenly outside our house.

Someone tall and determined climbed out and ran towards me. It wasn't Gran, it was Ned. Gran was in Kerry with her sister till Sunday. I'd forgotten that Ned was on his own. I'd totally forgotten.

I stood up. The breath that I'd been holding came out in one big yelp. I grabbed on to Ned's arm and for a second, he grabbed on to mine.

I pointed at the door and somehow, he managed to push it open and there was my mum lying pale and unconscious. He kneeled down beside her.

Nobody has to tell me what an idiot I am in a crisis. I stood, staring and frozen and it took me another while again to realise that Ned was talking to me.

'I've got her, Minty. I have your mum. Come on, it's OK. Out of the way.'

He was carrying her in his arms the way you carry a baby, except obviously Mum is a good bit bigger than that. Ned was strong and it didn't look like much of a struggle for him. There was a string of spit dribbling from Mum's mouth. Slowly, carefully he got her into the back of the van. He threw one of Gran's patchwork blankets over her, and lifted her head and put a bag under it for a pillow.

'You're OK,' he said to Mum, who didn't look like she was in the slightest bit OK.

He told me to get in.

'Is there someone else you need to phone?' he said as he barrelled along with his foot pressed hard on the accelerator and the sound of the engine squealing as though it was a living thing.

It can be stressful being friends with a lawless boy who doesn't care about boundaries or permission or the need for driving licences. But at that moment I guessed that if it wasn't for him, things would have ended up very differently.

21

It didn't come as a surprise to me that Ned was a fast and extremely precise driver.

We got to the hospital quickly and when we did, Ned shouted at the emergency doors. Two nurses and a doctor shifted Mum onto a trolley.

'Everything's under control now, we'll take her from here,' said one of them.

The coffee in the vending machine tasted like soup.

'Don't you think you should try to get a hold of your da? Don't you think you should at least tell him?' Ned asked.

'Look,' I said. 'I don't want to talk about my da, I mean my dad. I don't want to talk about my parents.'

It wasn't true. I did want to talk about them actually, I just didn't realise it, and Ned waited and eventually I told him how everything felt like it was falling apart.

'My dad's just got married to his new girlfriend. I mean he only met her a while ago, but anyway now they're married. I went to the wedding. I was the flower girl.'

Ned nodded his head.

'I saw them drive each other apart,' I told him. 'My mum is miserable. She's using up so much energy trying to pretend she's OK that she can't even see where she's going. No wonder she fell down the stairs.

'My parents told me everything was fine, Ned, but it wasn't fine. They were breaking up – and Dad knew he was leaving, but he never bothered to tell me, not until the last minute. They lied to me.

'My world used to be small and neat with everyone important to me located together in the same place.' I sniffed. 'Now it's complicated and random.'

'You don't need divorced parents to find that out. That's called living. It's called growing up,' he said.

For a moment I thought I might start to cry. The feeling came suddenly. I saw something, some flicker in Ned's face. He put his hand on my shoulder and then he took it away again but I was extra conscious for ages of the place on my body where his hand had been. It felt warm and sort of fuzzy.

'Hey, Minty, sorry, I didn't mean to make you sad.'

I told him I was sad anyway.

'Why won't anyone come and tell me how she is?' I wailed, and Ned said he'd get someone and I was to stay there and not lose the plot and I said I'd do my best.

He came back and told me the doctors were still assessing her and she needed X-rays and that these things take time.

'I'm going mad here, Ned. Talk to me about something. Something else.'

I'd started to shiver, which was weird seeing as it was hot there beside the humming vending machines.

Ned took off his jacket in one smooth move and threw it around my shoulders. And it was a consoling thing with its Nettleboggy herb and bonfire smell.

'OK then,' he said. 'Did I ever tell you about *my* mother?'

'No.'

'She came from a land far away and the day after she arrived in Ireland, she fell in love with my da, who, when he was alive, was the most charming man on earth.

'She had no interest in men, not until she met him. My gran used to say my da would charm an almond out of its shell. That's what he did to my mother, who wasn't prone to smiling on account of her being trained never to show her emotions in public. But my da made her smile and everyone could see that he'd cast a spell on her, and he was that one who was able to prove that she wasn't the ice princess everyone thought she was.

'They met at the Ballyross Race in the years when it used to be a grand event – when it was the race that brought many together, rich and poor, country and city, trainers, riders, owners. My da's name was Davy. Davy Buckley, the greatest rider the country has ever known. There was no one like him then. There's been no one like him since.

'Would you like to know what happened straight after my mother smiled at my father?'

'Yes,' I said. 'I would.'

'He fainted. Claimed the blood in his body rushed straight to his heart. He went temporarily blind. The world thought he was tough but he was always very sensitive to great beauty my da was. Very affected by it. He couldn't look at someone like my mother and not have had his senses overpowered.

'They married. My gran says they were like a storm – like ocean and land. He was a rock and she was a wave, Gran said, and when they crashed into each other there was mad noise and foam. They were from different worlds, but they had a lot in common.'

'Like what?' I asked

'A love of horses for one thing and a belief in courage,' he replied, flicking the elastic band on his wrist. 'Oh, and perfect singing voices.'

'What kinds of voices? What did they sound like?'

'I don't know.'

'What do you mean you don't know?'

'I can't remember hearing them.'

'Why?'

'I don't remember either of them. The only thing I know about them is from Gran. My da's dead now and my mother is gone.'

I wasn't surprised. I remembered Ned showing me his photo in the caravan. I remembered the dip of sadness in his voice when he'd talked about him.

'I'm sorry. That's lousy. I mean it's terrible,' I said, and he said, 'Yeah.'

Ned said Gran believed he'd got his spirit of defiance

and courage from his parents, but Ned said that was impossible because how can you get something from those you don't even remember.

This time Ned didn't look the slightest bit sad or lost when he told me that. And the way he said it made me feel as if it was a normal, unremarkable thing to have two parents, one like a rock and one like a wave, one of them dead, one of them gone. He swiped his hand through his hair and looked up at the ceiling.

I didn't find any of it hard to believe. Just looking at him it made sense. It was easy to think too that his mother had been a princess; his father the most charming man on earth.

A doctor with scruffy hair and white trainers walked down the corridor towards us.

'Hello, you two,' he said. 'Your mother's going to have a little surgery on account of her injury, but I'm glad to say that it's not going to take very long.'

Ned wouldn't stay. He said we were in the right place.

'I'm off. Good luck,' he said. 'I'll see you soon. Try not to worry.'

'Where are you going?'

'Eh, Minty, I'm in training, have you forgotten?'

'Oh yeah.'

'And as soon as you get out of here, you might come and give me a hand.'

I said I'd do what I could and he said great.

Meanwhile, though, I wasn't that happy about being left alone in the hospital waiting for my mum to get out of surgery. They told me I needed to call my dad. I had to unplug the drinks machine to charge my phone. Plus there was no Wi-Fi, and in situations like that there isn't anything else to do except think.

I thought of the horses that brought Ned's parents together. And I thought about my own mum and felt lucky she was still here – battered and bruised and broken, but here and living and with me, and part of my life. And it felt like I was being covered with new wisdom and the feeling was like someone wrapping a blanket around me. I sat waiting, surrounded by the tinkle and the clash of hospital noises. 'Mum, please be OK,' I said, to no one in particular. 'Mum, please get better.'

They were going to have to put pins in her thigh to straighten out her leg, which had been badly broken, but Mum was going to be OK.

You can break bones and those bones can heal. There was a lot else wrong with my mum. I'd known that for a long time.

I was waiting for her to wake up after the operation. Dad was supposed to be on his way by then. And I was a bit bored so I'd been looking at some pictures on my phone when Mum woke up.

'Oh, darling, I'm sorry,' was the first thing she said.

'It's OK, Mum, I'm just glad you're all right.'

I told her about what Ned had done in case she couldn't remember and she said I must say a very big thank you to him – and she shuddered to think, just like I did, what might have happened if he hadn't been there, what with the ambulance service under so much pressure these days, and with Dad so busy.

And it was then, when we happened to be on the subject of Dad, that she noticed my phone and the photo I happened to be looking at. It was a photo of Dad and Lindy's wedding.

'Hey,' she said. 'Hey, you never showed me those. Let me see.'

I couldn't have said no to an injured mother who'd just come round from an anaesthetic. It wouldn't have felt right. So, I peered over her shoulder as she swiped and gazed and then swiped and gazed again – at the miles of photographs in my phone of my dad kissing Lindy, of Dad and Lindy eating cake, of Dad and Lindy dancing, of every single one of Mum and Dad's old friends clapping in a circle around Dad and Lindy, and me and Lindy together in that awkward selfie, and of three of Mum and Dad's old friends standing behind a grinning Lindy, and of Dad holding a glass in the air and of Lindy throwing her bunch of flowers high up over her shoulder and these girls with pink feathers in their hair jumping at the same time to try to catch it.

I hadn't remembered taking that many photos. They

seemed to go on and on. Groggily, Mum swiped and she swiped and she swiped.

'Why do they want to catch the flowers, Mum?' I only asked the question because she'd gone so quiet and serious. I wanted us to talk about something – anything.

'It's a tradition,' she replied. 'The person who catches the flowers will be the next one to get married.'

'Why do they want that so badly?'

'I don't know, I just don't know, love.'

She was bent over in the bed, peering down and rocking a little bit – and that's when for a second I thought there might be some kind of leak in the hospital ceiling because a big wet splash landed on the screen of my phone.

It wasn't a leak. The wet splash had come from my mum.

And next thing she seemed to crumple under the covers, as if she was made of ice and she was melting, or as if she had been full of air and someone had stuck a pin into her.

'Oh, Mum,' I said.

'I'm fine,' she said for the millionth time.

'Stop saying that,' I said. 'Stop saying you are fine. You're not fine. I'm not fine. We're not fine. So just stop it. Stop it. Stop.'

And she did stop. And then she said I was right. She said she wasn't fine and she didn't feel cheerful and she was sad and lost and angry and scared.

The truth was coming out of her at last. And it felt like the first honest words she had spoken in a long time. I nearly hugged her but instead I held her hand for a minute, and I felt like she was coming back to me after all. That's what truth sometimes does.

Dad did come to the hospital but he stood outside the ward knocking so gently that it took me a while to realise he was there

'Mum, it's Dad,' I said.

'Don't, please, no,' she said. Call me shrewd, but I took that to mean she didn't want him to come in. So I went outside to talk to him.

'Dad, it's very late and she's tired, so why don't you try tomorrow?'

'Is she OK?'

'Her leg's going to be fine,' I said.

Before we left, we had a word with the nurses. They told us that anaesthesia can have a funny effect on your emotions.

Dad waited for me while I went in again, but by then Mum was asleep. And I kissed her, right on the forehead, as if I was the parent and as if she was the child.

It's not that easy to go to sleep when your mum is lying injured in a hospital bed with tears staining her face, and you're on a brand new sofa that belongs to your dad and your dad's new wife.

I couldn't stop thinking about Mum crying in her hospital bed as if she was lost in a dark place and nobody could find her.

Next day both Dad and I spoke to the doctor with the red hair and the pale face and the worn out trainers.

'Your wife is going to have to spend four weeks in traction.'

'Ex-wife,' I clarified, helpfully.

'Yes,' said the doctor. 'Right then, she'll need to keep her leg still while her body's natural powers of healing do the trick,' he said to my dad.

She wasn't going to be able to leave the hospital. She wasn't going to be able to get out of bed.

She was going to need a lot of help and support, he said. It was going to be a long road to recovery, and sometimes priorities come into sharp focus and everything else has to take a back seat.

For some reason, everyone kept looking at me like I was a bomb that was about to explode, and asking me how I was feeling and trying to get me to talk about how it had felt to find her.

They should probably have asked me other questions –

like how it feels to be in a one-parent family, how it feels
for my dad to have left, how it feels for him to be married
to someone else.

The day after that, Dad and Lindy had driven with me to
the hospital. Dad came to the ward. This time he said he
would prefer to see Mum before he left.

'I can't stay long,' was the first thing he said to her.
'Lindy's out in the car,' was the second.

'Are you OK?' he asked then.

'Does it seem as if I'm OK?' Mum said, not looking at
him.

Dad sighed.

'Listen, I think you need to get some help.'

She wanted to know why he'd bothered turning up if
the only thing he could do was give useless advice, and if
he just wanted to go away as soon as he'd arrived. There
was a table with wheels on it and a magazine on top of it. I
flicked through it, not reading anything, not even looking
at the pictures.

'I shouldn't have come,' he said to me as the two of us
walked down the corridor together.

'What do you want me to say to that, Dad? Just tell me
what you want to hear. What about, "Oh no, honestly, it

133

was nice of you to drop in"? Would that make you feel better about everything? Isn't that why you're here? To stop yourself from feeling guilty?'

'Minty, what do you want me to do?'

'That's an irrelevant question if ever I heard one,' I replied. 'Seeing as no matter what I want you to do, you go ahead and do what you want.'

Normally, saying things like that is a great way to start a fight, but in this case, it's not what happened.

We stood beside the glass doors, which kept opening and closing and he said, 'Minty, I know you're angry' and I said, 'Oh, do you? You honestly know that? Congratulations. Here, let me give you a medal.'

He kept on saying he should go, but he kept on not going and it would have been totally silent then for a while, if it hadn't been for the soft thudding of the automatic doors.

'You and your mum need to try to focus on the happy moments, Minty. There are good times in everyone's life, even when things don't feel so great.'

I wanted to say, Dad, if you have a bit of advice then make it practical, like 'charge your phone before you leave the house' or 'don't eat yellow snow'. I wanted to say, Hey, Dad, for your information, focusing on happy moments isn't that straightforward actually.

'Yeah, OK, thanks, Dad, whatever,' was the only thing I said in the end.

22

So Mum was going to get better, but she had a lot of getting better to do.

It was 'serendipitous' they said, that her injury had forced her to rest and meant she had to stay in hospital where she didn't have to take care of anything or worry about anything until she had recovered.

Traction involved hanging her leg from a giant elastic band on a frame from her bed and telling her that not only was she not to worry about anything or do anything for the next few weeks, she wasn't even supposed to move. For some, that might be an easy instruction to obey. For my mum, who normally couldn't sit still for a second, I reckoned it was going to be a good bit more difficult.

'What about Minty?' she kept on saying, and everyone kept assuring her I'd be perfectly fine, as if they knew.

'I'll be fine,' I started telling her too, because saying something over and over again can make it feel like a logical fact.

Dad came in again for a meeting with the doctors. It

wasn't any of his business how she was. It seemed wrong for him to be acting as though he was interested in her welfare now.

The nurses seemed delighted to hear that my mum had such a supportive ex-partner always on hand and always ready to be of assistance. Dad said that it would be no problem for me stay with him and Lindy for as long as I needed, while Mum recovered.

I took the opportunity to point out that it might be good for me to have some independence considering that – for everyone's information – in case it had escaped their notice, I wasn't a baby and I didn't need someone keeping me under surveillance twenty-four hours a day, thanks very much.

But the decision was already made. My job was to go home and pack anything else I was going to need. Dad's job was to clear out the spare room in his and Lindy's house so I didn't have to sleep on the sofa. It was actually a bonus as far as he was concerned, as Lindy had been on at him for ages to do something with that room.

Staying at Dad and Lindy's was a nightmare. I should have known – the clues had already been there. First, Lindy wasn't nearly as nice inside her house as she had been to me outside it. When I did the washing up, she took the plates and cutlery off the draining board and washed them again. And she followed me around the house with a coaster, and there was food in the fridge that was OK by her to eat, but there was other food in the same fridge that nobody was allowed near, but she never told me which was which so I was always making mistakes in that department.

Every couple of days she would say that she and Dad needed some 'quiet time', as if she thought I was three, and then they would go into their bedroom and shut the door and then I'd hear the lock being turned.

So obviously, that was completely disgusting.

Plus, the two of them did full frontal kissing in the kitchen while I was sitting at the table having a cup of tea or whatever.

'Dad,' I said, after I'd put up with four days of it. 'Seriously, I can live back at home. I can. You could look in on me every so often to make sure I'm all right, OK.'

But Dad was having none of it, and Lindy pretended she wouldn't hear of it either, even though I'm sure she'd have loved it.

'Don't you *want* to stay? Can't *this* be your home for a while?' Dad said with surprised high eyebrows and hurt in his eyes.

'It's fantastic here,' I lied. 'It's just that I don't want to be any trouble to anyone.'

'Don't be silly, Minty, you're no trouble whatsoever,' said Lindy, lifting up my mug of tea and wiping underneath with a cloth.

There were some good things though about having a mother in hospital and a newly-married dad. The main good thing was that nobody actually took that much notice of me. When Dad didn't see me, he thought I was with Mum and when Mum didn't see me, she thought I was with Dad. Sometimes that was kind of a good situation to be in.

The hospital was too hot. Dad and Lindy's was super-clean and I never knew where to sit down. School was OK, but for some reason, my friends were acting funny round me these days and I couldn't be bothered figuring out what that was about.

But Ned – I knew I could count on him. By far the nicest place to be was Nettlebog where everything was just the same as ever. And horses need exercise and care and Ned said he needed my help.

I'd learned everything about taking care of those horses, about feeding them and brushing them and leading them out of their shed and how to water them and I was Phoebe's person. It was obvious.

Every time I arrived, the way she nodded her head and swished her tail and made welcoming noises that meant she was thrilled to see me.

Ned said that Phoebe was ready for the Ballyross. He told me he'd put her name down, and then he told me he'd put mine down too.

'Me?' I whispered. 'Me in the Ballyross? You think I'd be able to do it?'

'Yes,' he said. 'You wouldn't just be able to. You'd be well in for a prize.'

I didn't believe him. I'd seen him dancing and flying on the back of Dagger. I knew the things he could do and I never imagined I could ever be anything like that.

'I don't think I can,' I said to him, feeling a wave of fear rising from somewhere deep.

'Not yet. But you will be once you've done the test, so come on, we'd better get going.'

'The test? What are you talking about?'

'Come with me and you'll find out. But hurry up. We're on a schedule.'

And I was glad, even though I hadn't a clue where he was taking me or what he had planned.

Ned helped me up onto Phoebe and he jumped onto Dagger in the way I'd grown to envy. He nudged his heels gently on Dagger's sides, and I did the same to Phoebe and our two brilliant horses started trotting along together. Full of joy they were, and a kind of anticipation that made me feel like the only one who didn't know what was happening next.

'Where are we going? What's the challenge?'

'Ha!' he said. 'It wouldn't be a proper test if I told you the answer to that. It's important – very important – that you don't know what to expect.'

'At least give me a clue.'

'The best way,' he shouted, 'to become a proper

Ballyross racer is to learn to go in one particular direction when practically everyone else in the whole world wants you to go in another.'

If I'd known what he meant, there's a chance I mightn't have gone with him.

Ned taught me a lot of things and one of the things he taught me is that you get to decide how to look at the world. You get to decide your version. It's up to you.

Everybody probably felt sorry for me. I might even have felt a bit sorry for myself. The nurses and doctors in the hospital deliberately put on solemn and sad faces when they looked at me – and kept on asking me how I was and I know it was because Mum and I had been abandoned by my dad and then my mum had fallen down the stairs.

You don't have to accept anyone else's version of you. It's much more exciting to invent your own version. You get to decide what that version is like.

We ended up on Callow Green. Callow Green is right in the heart of Ballyross. It has a very strict one-way system. They go completely mad if you even try to cross the road at the wrong place there, on account of the traffic and the tram that pulls into a stop every five minutes.

'Keep your nerve!' advised Ned.

Five times around the green I had to gallop. Five times wouldn't have been the challenge. Phoebe was meant to go fast, so that wasn't a problem either, and by then I wasn't a bad rider. The problem was that Ned made me gallop *the wrong way around*.

'Come on!' he said.

'We'll get into terrible trouble.'

'No, we won't.'

'It's dangerous,' I said.

'No, it's not, it's brave and it's a test and it will make you better at this, and isn't that what you want to be?'

There's no contest between a horse and a police car in the middle of town. We were long gone before anyone even knew what was happening. We hardly even heard the sirens.

We were back at Nettlebog drinking tea and Ned was laughing his head off and his gran was saying, 'Ha, here are two faces that have had an adventure today! What have you been up to?'

'Nothing much,' said Ned. 'I've just been teaching Minty and Phoebe to get to grips with their gallop.'

And Gran said, 'In that case, you must be starving, I'm sure you could do with some cheese and tomato sandwiches.'

We said that sounded great.

The little stove blazed away in the Buckley caravan and we drank the tea and we had the sandwiches and Gran told us stories about horse races long ago that Ned's father always won.

'Now what?' I said.

'Now,' replied Ned, 'you're ready.'

23

Everyone in our class ended up going to the Ballyross Race, even Brendan, and Serena came too, wobbling along the road in her little red car.

They say it's only the hooligans and scumbags that race in the Ballyross these days, and OK, Ned said, the riders might be a bit rough around the edges, and there might be a few scoundrels hanging around and most of them mightn't be from the right side of town or anything, but they still deserve respect. For keeping a brave and noble tradition alive.

The arena across the river was famous once, famous throughout the whole world. It used to be a glorious spectacle. Now it's run down and tangled. But a race is a race and when you commit you commit. Ballyross was my first, and it doesn't matter how many races you might run, you never forget your first one.

Afterwards, when anyone who had been there told their stories, it was as if they were telling some imaginary tale – something more like a fable or a myth. Their voices would grow low and much deeper than voices normally sound, and their eyes would look off in that dazed, dazzled way that humans sometimes have when they are remembering a moment of pure mad delight, or when they are thinking about a startling, secret place that they've never told anyone about.

It only lasted for like a minute and a half. The stories about it afterwards sometimes took a whole afternoon to tell. To us, though, and to the other riders, and to the superb horses we rode – in those wild short split seconds, time felt as if it had stood still.

When it came to the Ballyross Race, Ned Buckley was one thing that every one of the stories had in common.

Bigger-looking kids who I'd never seen had gathered before it started, and everyone shook hands and turned away to get their horses ready. I remember feeling very short suddenly, and puny and thin. Even Ned seemed small beside these riders who, Ned said, had come out of the woodwork to race him as soon as the word had got out. Ned was hard-faced and focused. If there was even a flicker of worry inside him, it definitely didn't show.

'Don't look them in the eyes,' he said to me under his breath, his lips hardly moving. 'When the time comes, jump up on Phoebe like you always do and don't look around, keep your eye on the course. Keep looking straight ahead. You've already passed the test. You've galloped with sirens blaring behind you – remember that. This will be pure easy in comparison.

'Listen, Minty, if you want a chance of winning – here is what you have to do: remove the longing from your heart. Just focus on the ride. The human race plays tricks on itself every minute, every day, but especially in situations like this. Longing for things and hoping for things and wanting things. Don't think about the finish line. Be loyal to the moment. The rest will look after itself.'

I'd been right. Ned knew things that no one else knew. It felt good that he was explaining some of those things to me.

There were taunts from the crowd and twitchy horses flicking their tails and grunting and trampling on the grass.

'Hey, hey, Ned Buckley, good to see you, sir! How are you getting on with the books? Can you do your sums now? Have they taught you how to count? Can you read yet?'

I knew that red-haired, round-faced guy. It was Martin Cassidy. His family hadn't moved away after all. Or if they had, they'd come back for this. From the way he was warming up, it seemed his coccyx had made a complete recovery.

'So you've turned up. You mustn't have learned much since I saw you last, if you think you've a chance,' snickered Martin.

Ned spat on the ground and looked past Martin as if he wasn't there.

I tried to focus just on me and on Phoebe, but every comment, every bellow, every cheer from the crowd made me feel as if I might lose my balance.

'Remember what I said, Minty,' Ned whispered. 'They'll try to rattle you. But no one can do that if you don't let them.'

'So keep looking straight ahead,' Ned repeated. 'It's a game. You get to decide how it's played, not them.'

But the other racers didn't bounce in the air as their horses jittered at the start line – not like I felt I was doing.

Ned jumped up on Dagger and I was still for a moment with the horror you sometimes get when you suddenly feel as out of place as it's possible to feel.

'What? What is it?'

'I don't belong here,' I replied. 'I don't think I can do this. It's not like I'm ever going to win.'

'Minty,' he said. 'Do you want this lot to win before the race has even started?'

I took a few breaths.

'No.'

'Right then, are you still in?'

'I'm in, Ned. I still am.'

And he said, 'Good stuff. Of course you are.'

Not only was Brendan here, but apparently, he had the makings of an excellent bookie. He'd spent the morning introducing himself to everyone and carrying a scraggy battered notebook. The stub of a pencil was tucked behind his ear. He was giving fifty to one on Ned. Six hundred to one on me.

'Take no notice of the odds, they are nothing – just a number plucked from a dreamer's head. They only mean something if you let them.

'This is going to belong to the person who deserves it and the person who deserves it is the person who keeps their head.'

The countdown was on. There was no more time for talking. A tiny boy flung his arm in the air and Ned's eyes fixed on a short space in front. High and brave he galloped, clinging on to Dagger's brilliant shiny mane. No saddle. No stirrups. No fear.

I charged after him.

A lot of riders don't remember anything about the races that they run and that's true of me for the beginning of the Ballyross. But I'll probably remember the final stretch for ever. Every thump and thud. Every roar and crash.

I could see from the shape of Ned's crouching body that he didn't hear any of it. There was a kind of sound coming up off everyone that wasn't like ordinary voices, even though that's what it was made of.

I stayed behind him the whole way. I didn't see any of the others. I didn't know how far behind we'd left them.

Ned won the Ballyross Race. I came second, and as we crossed the finish line, great mobs surged forwards to shake our hands and pat our horses.

Brendan was pale with astonishment and defeat, as if he'd been a rider too. Apparently he lost his shirt.

It turns out lots of people had put their money on Ned after all. It turns out that Brendan was one of the only people who didn't think he had a chance.

Soon Martin was shouting across to us and I thought I might have been imagining it, but from where I was, it looked as if there were actual tears in his eyes.

'Ned Buckley and that bit of a girl?' he kept roaring in disbelief. 'Them and their scabby-looking horses?'

Ned had swung off Dagger and was walking slowly in Martin's direction.

'Hard luck, Marty.' Ned held out his hand. This time it was Martin who spat on the ground. He glowered there for a second. Then he was surrounded by a clump of his gang who stared at us before they melted back into the crowd.

Orla had the video on YouTube within a couple of hours. By the time we got to it, there'd already been one thousand and thirteen views.

'We're going to be famous,' I said.

'You already are,' replied Dougie, looking at us and then looking at the screen. There'd been a reporter. From a TV station. They'd made a news clip about us.

Horses, ten of them – the wildest, snortiest-looking animals you're ever likely to see – danced and fidgeted at the start line. There was smoke coming out of their noses

148

as if it was winter. A tiny, twitchy-looking boy in a T-shirt held a white rag, as two other bigger boys, swaggering with the satisfaction and assuredness of authority, kept an eye on the jumpy row of competitors – glaring, pointing, shouting at the riders to stay behind the line, signalling to each other about the countdown.

Mobs everywhere. In the ditches next to the muddy course; in the crooked trees that lined the route. Leaning out of broken windows in the tall towers of the flats nearby. Hanging off lampposts and drainpipes, waiting for the white flag to be raised in the air and for the race to begin.

A hush fell. And it was a sacred moment, except for the distant wail of a siren echoing in the air. The stomping of the row of tense horses sounded like the beating of a drum.

The boy in the T-shirt raised his hand and waved the rag as high in the air as he could manage.

With a scuffle and a trample, the racers were off, and the quietness that gripped everyone in the minutes leading to this moment evaporated into an unruly roar.

The video caught Ned's face for a moment, as he and his horse sped by, and you could see that he was doing the things he told me to do: not wishing or hoping or longing for anything, just being on his horse. Just doing the best he could do. I've watched that video a good few times now, and right at the edge of the crowd you can see Serena Serralunga in a beautiful suit cheering and clapping and jumping up and down.

The camera juddered along beside the horses and it was Ned who stayed in front, and it was Ned and his horse who flew ahead of the scrabbling others, the others who never had a chance. The camera kept its focus on Ned and Dagger till the end, as if it wasn't interested in anyone else – right until Ned won, and until he was surrounded by the hysterical crowd.

There was a kind of heaven in the moments of breathlessness and exhaustion that followed. I didn't want to talk to anyone else or smile at anyone else or look at anyone else. Only Ned.

'Those horses. They're a gift. They're magic, I'm telling you.'

'You don't have to tell me,' he replied. 'I know that already. They'd be brilliant anyway, even if we hadn't won.'

I felt something for the first time ever in my life. Gran explained to us later that the feeling I had was called 'the grace of the underdog', which is an airy mood that you get when you come second in a race that everyone thought you hadn't a chance of even finishing.

'That was something else, wasn't it?'

'Yes,' I said. 'It was.'

'Our horses are proper miracles.'

'Yeah, and you and your miracle won.'

'True, but I was sweating it there for a while. I thought you were going to beat me.'

'I never had a chance.'

We were heroes when we got back to school and Serena thought so too.

Everyone crowded around us. Dougie ruffled Ned's hair, and he and Mark Baker lifted Ned, and Ned was too amazed to resist. And then Orla and Laura lifted me too. Up onto the shoulders of our classmates we rose and they carried us around, high and wobbly. I could see dust and dead flies and a stranded paper aeroplane on the sills of the tall windows and I could see right out to the car park and the yard.

Ned was right. This was going to be another story that I would be able to tell. Once you have a story, no matter what happens after it, nobody can take it away from you.

Between the whooping and the clapping, I looked over at Ned, who looked back at me and gave me one of his smiles. Everyone kept cheering for quite a long time and we stayed there like that, lifted up high and I kept looking at him and his face. His lovely face.

I should have known it wasn't going to last. We were called into Mr Carmody's office. He more or less laid the blame for everything at Ned's feet. He said he had been watching the developing dynamics, first with concern and then with increasing alarm. He had heard the whole story, so there wasn't any point in us trying to keep anything from him, just in case we thought there was.

He told us that he was very disturbed by recent events. Parents had been in contact with him and they had begun to say that Ned Buckley was a seriously bad influence. 'Poisonous,' is what he said.

'There is a student, a student who will remain nameless, but who has been lured into extremely unsavoury activity as a direct result of this race that the two of you rode in. His father got the whole thing out of him. Gambling, Minty, can you imagine such a thing? He lost a substantial amount of money. Money that he was supposed to have been saving for his summer holidays.'

I didn't mind that Mr Carmody was so angry. I mean I got it – I understood. But it was galling how Ned and me were getting the blame for Brendan's betting streak, which was nothing to do with us.

'If you're talking about the person I think you're talking about, then you should know that he would lose his shirt on a race between two flies crawling up a wall,' Ned said. We tried not to laugh, but we couldn't help it.

When a bad influence begins to breathe its toxic fumes from student to student, bad things start to happen, and Mr Carmody wanted Ned to know that he wasn't going to tolerate it.

'This time, Minty, I am going to have to speak to your parents.' He sighed, looking at me carefully now, imagining, I suppose, that this was going to make me crumble.

'My mum's in hospital recovering from surgery and my dad's at home, but to be quite honest with you, mentally he's still on a honeymoon that looks like it may actually go on for ever, so having a word with them is possibly going to be a bit inconvenient,' I said.

Whatever was convenient or inconvenient, Mr Carmody replied, one thing was certain and that was that 'the horse situation' was 'not sustainable'.

He began to sharpen a pencil with a machine on his desk. It made a surprisingly loud drilling noise that drowned some of his words. He took the pencil out of the machine, looked at its pointy tip, held it up to his face and blew. A tiny yellowish dust cloud of shavings sprinkled across the desk.

'Minty, you're normally a reliable student, but something seems to have happened to you recently, and you need to know that nobody is bigger than the rules.

'When I meet your parents, I'll have to discuss a variety of options and courses of action. I'll be ringing them in the morning.'

If Mr Carmody rang my dad, he wasn't going to answer. He never answered. The signal was terrible in the hospital, and if he tried to get through to the ward my mum was on, the nurses would keep him waiting on the line for, like, half an hour, and he'd probably give up.

'Look, OK, on second thoughts, you're totally right, Mr Carmody,' I said, putting on the most apologetic face I could manage. 'I definitely think you should ring them.'

24

Next morning there was an unusual noise in the corridor – the kind that makes you know something is going on before you know what it is.

Serena was gone.

'What's happened to Serena?' Laura asked. You could see she was trying to be cool about it, but she and everyone else looked confused, waiting for the answer.

Mr Carmody wasn't going to be drawn. She'd left the school and she wouldn't be coming back, and that was that.

No note, no warning.

'But we didn't get a chance to say goodbye!' said Dougie, who usually never looked as sad as he did just then.

'Where has she gone?' asked Orla.

'Where every visitor here goes, sooner or later, back to where she came from,' said Brendan.

It was a day of unpredictable things. That evening, Mum rang me at Dad's. The signal sounded disturbingly great. She said she was much better. It was about time she got up and on with the rest of her life, she said.

'I'm strong again and my doctors have told me there's nothing stopping me from coming straight home, whenever I'm ready.'

This time I kind of felt that maybe she was. Or that if she wasn't, she was going to be.

'Oh, yes, and by the way, another thing, what does Mr Carmody want to see me for exactly?' she asked.

'I've no idea,' I said.

They'd have found out anyway.

Ned had rung to tell me to turn on Sky. 'We're an international news item, Minty!' I'd legged it to Dad and Lindy's sofa with the remote control.

'Once a high profile, respectable local event, now unknown to many of the members of mainstream society, the race remains a phenomenon in this area,' the reporter said, *'a status symbol among certain types of youth of this small town of Ballyross. Children wanting to be able to control powerful dangerous animals . . . There's a lot of symbolism wrapped up in the rituals of these races . . . You have to see it in context . . . These kids seek empowerment. They seek control in a world that often feels chaotic and unstable, in a place where they don't feel they call the shots.*

This type of racing is an antidote for them . . . When they race you see, they feel like kings.'

And just then I heard the clicky slide of the key in the door. It was Dad. There was someone behind him, but it wasn't Lindy. It was Mum. Hobbling in behind him with a grey face. I turned off the TV.

'Mum, what are you doing here?'

Next thing Dad was standing right beside her and for a moment I had this mad feeling that they were going to tell me they'd got back together, but of course it wasn't anything like that.

'Sit down, both of you.' I forced a smile. 'You're making me nervous.'

They sat side by side, touching almost but not quite at the end of the sofa, looking at me as if they were about to break some bad news.

And then, in unison, they went crazy.

'We had no idea how wild you had become . . .

'Look, I know things haven't been easy, and we've been through a lot and everything . . .'

'But, Minty, we can't put up with this. We're very concerned.'

They told me what Mr Carmody had said about my behaviour – how Ned and I had been ringleaders. We had lured – *lured* – others into the grounds of the old racing arena beside the ruined factory in Nettlebog where illegal racing of wild horses and gambling had taken place. We'd whipped the others in the school into a fever of defiance and delinquency.

'Mum, Dad, listen that's not true. You couldn't lure anyone in my class anywhere. They're not those kinds of kids, especially not Brendan Kirby, who only ever does exactly what he wants to do. They went to the Ballyross Race of their own accord. Mr Carmody hasn't a clue. Serena Serralunga was the best teacher we ever had. He's got everything completely wrong.'

It was obvious they weren't even listening to me.

I'd brought the school into disrepute they went on. A YouTube clip of the whole thing had already gone viral. The school's reputation was being undermined, quite apart from the danger I was posing to myself and others.

Mr Carmody had told them how they were going to have to think long and hard about what was best for me. He told them that he had to consider the welfare of the whole school and that taking the greater good into account was a very important part of his job – and what a harmful influence we had become. Me and Ned Buckley.

'And I wouldn't mind, but that's not even the whole of it, Minty,' my dad had said, studying his fingernails and then looking at me. 'We might have been able to put this down to a couple of bad choices, if it hadn't been for something else we know.'

'What?' I said. 'What do you know?'

'I got a phone call, Minty, a phone call from Petie Farrell's wife, who happened to be on Callow Green some weeks ago. She said she saw you with a ragged-looking boy, who I can only assume is Ned.'

Mum's eyes got rounder and she put her hand up to her mouth.

'She thought her eyes were deceiving her. She saw *you* with this boy – *galloping* on horses without saddles, the wrong way around Callow Green, being followed by a police car with the siren blaring. Minty, talk to me, can this possibly be true?'

'Mum,' I began to plead. 'You know Ned. You know the person he is.' But Dad had moved into questioning mode.

'Have you any idea how *wrong* that behaviour is? What in heaven's name possessed you to do such a thing?'

I told them I did it because it made me feel better. It made me feel good. It made me feel great.

They said I should have told them. They said they shouldn't have had to hear this kind of thing from anyone else. They said I shouldn't have kept this to myself. And I said yeah, there are lots of things that you shouldn't keep to yourself, but for some reason you do.

They were both sitting with grave, stony faces, and then, in a very dejected, slow voice, my dad said, 'Minty, how *on earth* could doing something like that make you feel better about anything? What's so bad about your life that you need to behave in such a way?'

And right after that is when I broke the remote control. It was the nearest thing to me. I picked it up and whacked it against the wall and parts of it snapped off and flew back into my face like shrapnel.

'Minty,' said Dad.

Mum said she wasn't going to have a conversation when everyone was so angry, but I knew obviously that she meant me. She hauled herself up on her crutches and began to limp towards the door.

'Stay in the room! Stop running away from everything. Stay here and face me,' I screamed at her.

'Minty, please, that's very unfair,' said Dad.

'Unfair? You're the one who's let me down, let us both down and you talk to me about being unfair! I hope you're happy for ruining my life.'

'Minty, I haven't ruined your life. That's not true. I'm trying very hard to figure this out, to make this work.'

'Yeah, well it's not working.'

I went on for another bit about how I hated Lindy and how I had no idea why he married her and how I only went to the wedding to keep everyone happy. I said that from then on I was going to look after myself, because one thing was for sure, I couldn't rely on anyone else. And I said a whole load of other things and then I began to cry.

'Minty, I need you to listen carefully now, because this is what is going to happen. I am going to leave the room to talk to your mother. When we both come back, we expect you to be fully calmed down.'

I kicked the remains of the remote control around the place. I screamed. My parents have this disturbing ability to behave as though they're reasonable and composed in the face of furious despair.

They left me there for fifteen minutes and in a funny way, it kind of worked. The mountain of rage shrank a little, and when it did, they came back in. Mum had made a pot of Camomile tea, as if that was the solution to everything.

They told me there was only one thing for it and whether I liked it or not they knew it was the right decision. The decision was that I wasn't allowed to see Ned any more. Ned Buckley was forbidden.

'What are the two of you even talking about?'

'Minty, Ned has been the cause of a whole range of problems and you must know what we are talking about.'

'No, I don't. What has he done? He races in very hard competitive races. Is there anything wrong with that? The only thing he's guilty of is winning them.'

Then Mum put on this annoying face that she does when she's trying to explain something that she thinks you're having difficulty understanding. 'Minty, Ned is the kind of boy that may not be that good for you. I'm going to tell you something about him now that's highly confidential, and I'm only telling you because I think you need to know. I think it will explain a lot to you.'

'What?'

'Darling, he's desperately disadvantaged. He's only just learning how to read.'

'Why would I even care about something like that?' I wailed. 'Why is that a reason I can't be friends with him?'

'Minty, he's just not like you. He's different from anyone

160

else at your school. He has challenges and disadvantages and someone like that is not always good for you, no matter what you think of him, no matter how much you like him. Minty, don't you understand what we're talking about here? We are talking about what's best for you.'

'Ha!' My laugh felt bitter and grown-up. 'What's best for me? What a complete joke. You have no right. It's not up to you. It's none of your business – either of you. You don't have a right to tell me who I can and can't be friends with.'

And together in something that sounded like a single voice, they said, 'We do.'

25

'It's because he lives in a caravan, that's it, isn't it?'

'No, that's absolutely not it. It's to do with the fact that the boy appears to be some kind of a delinquent and since you've met him, so it seems, do you.'

'You don't even appreciate what's wrong with the way you have been behaving.'

'You're going to have to trust us and work with us, OK?'

'Ned Buckley isn't a delinquent. He is braver and kinder than anybody I've met.'

'He ranges around the place on those wild horses, Minty, can you not see how awfully inadvisable that is? He drives his grandmother's van. It's illegal. He's no respect for the law.'

'I can't believe you're even saying that! He only did that because it was an emergency, don't you remember? To save you, to get you to the hospital?'

'You have to put this in context.'

I told them I didn't have to put anything in context. I told them that was a ridiculous thing to say.

This was the first thing they'd been united about anything for a very long time, and I already knew I was powerless to change their minds. It felt like a giant door swinging closed and getting locked. I could almost hear it. A huge thing creaking into place with a great bang, and a loud rasp, and a hard slam.

I texted Ned.

My parents don't want me 2 c u nymore

He texted back.

What u goin 2 do?

I'm comin over

After I got there, he and I didn't speak for a very long time.

'They're probably right, you know. There are loads of things about me you don't know.'

I lay on the springy ground of Nettlebog. Ned sat beside me with his elbows on his knees looking at the grass. Not looking at me.

'This world is full of people who don't understand anything,' I said.

'Ah, Minty. Don't be so hard on the human race – it's not that bad,' he said, flicking a stick across the grass.

'Easy for you to say,' I said.

'Not as easy as you think,' he replied.

26

The news was out. Ned was being expelled. Mr Carmody had told Mr Doyle and Mr Doyle had told Mr Kirby who told Brendan, who told us.

I texted him from under my desk:

Where u?

At hom

Carmody expelled u

I know

I'm goin 2 defend u. Doin my bst.

Gud 4 u. Keep me posted.

I didn't want to go to a school that Ned wasn't in. I guess I hadn't realised how much I didn't want that until this moment.

Mr Carmody had some more news for us. I always knew by the way he wiggled his fingers together and waited for the hush to rise.

'Of course I have been able to clamp down on the behaviour at Nettlebog and at least we shouldn't expect any more trouble of . . . shall we say . . . an equine nature.'

'What does that mean?' I said, but already I could feel the heat in my face turning to cold.

He smiled a thin smile. 'I've organised it with Mr Kirby at the council. He's sending a team to Nettlebog to confiscate those horses.'

And that's when, not listening to his shouts or his orders, I got up and left.

Everything changes a little bit when you walk through the Nettlebog archway with its tangled curves and its twisted branches. I could always feel something happening to me when I passed through. I got strength in my legs. Whatever it was, it gave me power. It gave me courage.

I didn't stop cycling till I got to the bottom of Nettlebog Lane.

'You've got to get away,' I gasped at the caravan door out of breath and full of purpose.

'Ah, deary, what do you mean?'

'Someone's coming down here to take the horses off you!'

'Ha no, I don't think so,' Gran said and it was obvious she had no idea of the emergency we were in the middle of.

'Gran, listen! Listen to me.'

'Lovey, calm yourself. They'd never take those horses, I'd make sure they never would.'

'I've always been able to sort them out.' She smiled.

'There's no time,' I said. 'You don't understand.'

Ned was in a panic already, running to the shed. But Gran seemed to be in a fog. She sighed and said, 'Minty, Ned, will you come in or go out, but that draught would cut the legs off you, so if you don't mind, I'll be shutting the door.' She went back inside, and I couldn't stand there doing nothing, so I started knocking and hammering and shouting for her to come out again. And I was being so noisy and loud that I hadn't even heard the sounds behind me. I turned around and there was a car parked beside Gran's old van, and there were two men getting out of it and the car had 'County Council' woven into a crest on the side of it.

'Ned Buckley,' said the council guy. 'We have to take the horses. You know that's what we have to do.'

Ned was standing in front of the shed. He had a crazy look on his face, but at the same time, it didn't look as though he had heard.

Gran hurried out and said nobody was to do anything. She told me to keep Ned under control, and she told the council men to wait.

'Nobody is to think about going near those horses. I

have everything we need somewhere in here,' she said, pointing back at the caravan and then dashing back inside.

'Gran, what are you doing?'

I looked in at the window and saw Gran tearing the lids off the tin boxes and lifting the lids of the wooden boxes and tossing the coloured blankets in the air.

'Go away,' shouted Ned to the men. 'You're frightening my gran and you've no right to be here.'

'Ned, stop,' I said. 'Gran's sorting it out. She'll fix it. You've just got to keep your head till she finds the papers.'

'Ned Buckley, on the basis of several complaints and in accordance with the byelaws of Ballyross town . . .'

I was afraid.

'Listen, everyone,' I interrupted, 'this whole thing is a misunderstanding. Mrs Buckley has the paperwork – she's just . . . locating it . . . you can't do anything to her or to the horses. She has everything she needs to show you – this is wrong.'

None of them even looked as if they'd heard a word I'd said. I began to whisper.

'You can't tell Ned you're taking his horses away.'

'We can. It's the rules,' said one of them.

'OK, then, even if it is, please don't. Don't tell him that's what you're here to do because if you do, something's going to happen.'

'What will happen?' asked the man.

'I don't know. Something dreadful.'

27

'**M**inty,' he shouted. 'Minty, we've got to get them out of here.'

Everyone was looking at us now.

'Run! Minty, quick. Come on! Didn't you hear what they said? You need to get over here.'

I knew nobody was going to be able to stop him. And I was right. Ned loved those horses with a love that made him desperate and grim. They'd taught him things that he might have learned from humans, but the truth was, he didn't have that many humans in his life.

Dagger and Phoebe were afraid, I could see that too, but they'd have gone anywhere with Ned and they'd have done anything he said.

Horses understand things, tiny changes in the voices of the humans they love, the slightest shift in the way someone's face is arranged. They can feel the way your body tenses ever so slightly when you're even a small bit nervous. To a horse that can feel like a thunderstorm. They see and feel things that humans usually never spot.

I was frozen as I watched. It didn't look like he could escape with everyone surrounding him like that and the river to his back. Ned called the horses, and the horses launched themselves into the water, as everyone stood staring. It was Ned who was in control now.

'Go on, go on,' he shouted and the horses kept plunging and snorting deeper and deeper. He ran and leaped onto his tyre-swing and he hauled himself high up over the water, and jumped down onto Dagger's back.

'Come on, Minty, I need you,' he roared.

I had another story then and so did everybody else – the story of the moment I followed Ned, the moment I swung myself off the tyre, just as he had done, the moment I landed on Phoebe and went after Ned across the river. Everyone was watching us, those men who thought they were the ones with the power. The only thing they did then was stand gawping as we disappeared, as we scrambled up the bank on the other side, and as we jumped over the gorse bushes as if we had wings.

The sirens were blaring and the chase was on and there's an ordinary bridge to the other side of the river, and it didn't take them long. We kept on galloping, but we could hear them coming.

'Ned, where are we going?'

The bushes were higher here, and we didn't know this side of the river nearly as well as the Nettlebog side, and anyway Ned wasn't answering me. He was up ahead gripping on to Dagger and even if I'd asked him to wait it wouldn't have made any difference.

I kept on feeling that something awful was going to happen and there wasn't going to be anything I could do to stop it except try to keep up, except try to stay with him.

He slipped out of view and I said, 'Come on, Pheebs, faster, you can do it.' But Phoebe knew before I did, because there was something in her that began to slow and her step became gentler and her ears pricked to hear it. The screech. The smash.

There are some things that nobody can do anything about and it doesn't matter how much they try, and sometimes it doesn't matter how strong their will is or how brave they are.

Dagger was lying on the rocky ground and Ned lay his head on Dagger's and he cried. His whole body cried, and everyone else stood there looking at him.

I didn't want anyone to hear the noise Ned was making, and I won't describe it because describing it would dishonour him, and I would never want to do that.

But everyone came, and they heard anyway.

Soon the official-looking men had their notebooks open, a whole crowd was standing by with phones blinking. The sirens screamed in my head.

I don't think he'd mind me saying that he told his horse that he was very sorry. He said everything had been his fault.

He stayed with Dagger for a long time and he didn't seem to notice the others standing there watching. And he didn't care. Nobody had the heart to take him away and I don't think anyone could have, even if they'd tried. I remember how he didn't look like himself. He looked alone. He looked like someone does when nobody's on their side. He was suddenly very small, suddenly lost. He just looked like a little kid.

'Leave me alone and leave my horses alone. We're all right,' he said, smearing something that was coming from his nose and leaving a red streak across his arm. It was blood. Ned's eyes rolled back. He fell against me and slid to the ground.

Dagger moved. He thrashed for a while but then he struggled to his feet.

'Ned, Dagger's OK. He's OK. Ned,' I said. 'You're right about them, Ned. It would take more than a stumble on rocky ground to keep Dagger down.'

This time it was Ned who wasn't moving.

Dagger stood beside Ned's shaking body, shivering and

neighing in a way that sounded as if he might have been crying himself.

It took me and five others to move Dagger out of the way to make room for the ambulance.

Don't ask me how Dad found out, but there he was in the middle of it, saying enough was enough and that he was taking me home. According to him, I was lucky to be alive and this had been the most frightening thing that had ever happened and what's more it was proof that everything he and Mum had said was right.

'Dad, there are a lot of things I've been trying to forgive you for,' I said, 'but if you don't take me to hospital to make sure Ned's OK right now, that's something I'll never forgive you for. Never, do you understand me?'

And maybe I'll never know the exact reason for this either, but for the first time in a very long time, Dad looked as if he was listening to me, and even more amazingly, he did what I'd asked him to do.

I ran down the corridors of the hospital and I could hear my breathing and the clumping of my own steps.

'I need to see Ned Buckley,' my words came out in sobs.

'What relation are you to the patient?' asked the nurse in Admissions.

'What relation am I to the patient? What relation?' I inhaled very deeply and I felt the way I imagine everyone must feel when they are about to say something important, something that matters.

'Friend,' I said. 'Best friend.'

I said it three or four times as if it needed to be said, as if I needed everyone to hear it and to know it – as if I was announcing it to the whole world.

Gran was there already, sitting by Ned's bed. She'd sorted everything out. The horses were fine. The 'A bit shook' but no permanent damage. They were at the vet's stables being taken care of.

'Are they going to take them away?' I asked.

'They are on my eye,' she replied, which meant no they weren't.

'Gran Buckley has never been in illegal possession of anything,' she said, furious and proud. 'Those council boys may not realise it, but they are going to be in serious trouble for what they have done.'

Gran had every one of the correct papers, of course she did. It had taken her a while to find them but they were there – the vet's endorsements and certificates, and it's true that in Nettlebog it's illegal for boys to own horses, but Gran was the official owner of Dagger and Phoebe. Everything was in order and there was nothing else that needed to be done except give those upstarts from the council a complete dressing down.

'They'll be sorry,' she whispered, talking to herself. 'No one gets away with that kind of nonsense, not when it comes to my boy and his horses. I won't have it.'

Even though she was smiling, I could see she was still raging – but some rage feels like a safe place. Some rage knows what it's talking about and it feels as if it is going to sort everything out. And that's what Gran's was like. Good anger. Righteous and true.

Gran said she was sure we'd loads of things to talk about. And when Ned looked at me, I thought I saw even more new things in him that I'd never seen before.

It took Ned's gran a long time to calm down. She was sick of it, she said. She'd a good mind to go to the top guy at the council and demand an apology. She said she'd been told by that teacher, Serena, that her grandson honoured an ancient tradition.

She said Serena had talked to her after the race, and she'd extended an open invitation to Ned to be her guest in Siena any time in the future. 'Which other citizen of Ballyross with their airs and graces, which of them can say they've been invited to Siena?'

And then a new courage grew inside us both and we began our serious conversation – the one that made us believe that we could go to Siena. Not in our dreams but now, here. In real life.

It's bizarre when you think about it. How someone can have a conversation, which turns into a possibility, which eventually becomes a rock-solid plan. That's basically what happened. And it's how a vague dream about Ned's trip to Italy turned into a definite thing.

'I'll only go on one condition,' he said.

'What condition is that?'

'If you come with me.'

28

Ever since Serena had begun to explain about the Palio, Ned had decided he was going to go to Siena anyway, and he never changed his mind about wanting me to come too and so that is why we planned the trip together.

Gran was our ally and it seemed like a minor miracle, but my parents had got softer about what they liked to call 'the Ned Buckley issue'. They'd been to see a counsellor who'd told them that making someone forbidden is a sure way of increasing their attraction, and because of this they told me they were willing to cooperate too. They Skyped Serena to confirm that the invitation was genuine. Ned used his Ballyross prize money for the flights and we booked them with my dad's credit card from one of the library PCs early one Saturday morning in June.

Gran took us to the airport in her rusty white van.

Serena was waiting for us in Pisa, as sparkly and magic as she'd always been. It was great to see her. She said ordinarily when she had visitors who fly into this airport, she takes them to see the leaning tower, but this was no ordinary day, and this was no ordinary visit, and there was no time.

'Welcome and thank you,' she said 'for doing me the honour of this visit. You will never know how much this matters.'

We brought our bags in. She showed us to our enormous rooms. She told us she'd be waiting downstairs with food when we were ready.

Serena's sandwiches were delicious. Fresh mozzarella, basil, deep red tomatoes. The colours of the Italian flag.

She had a stable full of horses and she had a niece called Lucia who shook our hands and kissed us on both cheeks and said she was thrilled finally to meet us. She knew we'd galloped to school one day on horses called Dagger and Phoebe. She knew my mum had broken her leg and gone to hospital. She said Serena thought we were two of the greatest students she'd ever taught. I was amazed.

'I know I left so suddenly, and I am sorry for that,' Serena said, 'but I felt sure I was going to make things worse.'

Just as she had said, Serena was from a noble Italian family. They owned one of the buildings in the Piazza del Campo and there was a balcony on it, from where we were going to see the race. And if we didn't want to miss it, we'd better get going.

We turned down a narrow cobbled road and there we were in the fan-shaped square. It was glorious, and the ancient clock tower of red and creamy stone loomed high above.

It's true. Ned and I have been there and we've seen it.

Ned holds out his hand as we step onto the balcony, and there is nothing do to but hold mine out too and then we are shaking hands and we aren't letting go, so I guess we are holding hands and then he pulls me towards him and I press my face into his neck and I can smell him – not bonfire any more but cloves and mint – and if belief has a smell, then that's what Ned smells of. I breathe him in and I'm wrapped up in another new feeling that doesn't have a name.

'Hello,' I say as if I haven't seen him for ages.

'Hello yourself,' he replies. And he looks at me and his dark eyes stay on me. He's the only still person in the whole of the fidgety, swelling, seething Piazza del Campo and I'm seeing the whole lot of him, not just the outside. And he's seeing the whole lot of me too. He sees the little kid and the angry girl and the believer and the reckless rider and the courage and the fear and the sadness, everything that is in me.

The rustle and roar is getting louder now. Something is changing here in the Piazza del Campo. Everything feels as if it's getting closer.

'Look,' Ned says.

We both look down at the square, at the Fantini and the banners and the colours and the bellowing crowd.

He has that sureness in his eyes and there are things that Ned is right about that nobody else understands. When the Palio is over, there is a very good chance I'm going to kiss him.

If you've been to the Palio there are things you can never forget. The way the horses dance at the starting line ready to run. The way everyone waits for the loaded moment when the race is going to begin. We're waiting for it too, and we're ready and we know it's coming.

And it's better and brighter and finer than anything I've seen.

I don't know what Ned is thinking, but I imagine maybe he's thinking the same as me. One day it could be us. As strong and fast and fearless as the Fantini. We will have the same expressions on our faces – fixed and steady – we will be ready to give it everything. Everything we have.

The balcony gets full and everyone squashes us up together with the jostle and the loudness and the buzz.

I see the way Ned's eyebrows do that little lift and his eyelashes blink and I can see him saying something.

'Listen, Minty, I . . .' he shouts, but the crowd roars louder than ever.

'What? What did you say?'

Ned points down at the man in the white shirt.

Even though we're waiting for it, the bang of the gun makes us jump.

And the horses, those brilliant horses, strong and sleek and loyal to the moment – they're off.

Acknowledgements

I thank my wonderful editor Fiona Kennedy for her wisdom, expertise and good cheer, which are constant sources of gladness to me.

Jo Unwin possesses magic that affects everyone she meets. She took me on a mini writing holiday last summer. Those four days reminded me how simple things like generosity and nourishment are such powerful foundations for wellbeing and creativity. Thanks also to Dido Crosby and Anne Buchanan for the delightful hospitality.

Thanks to my early readers, Ben Moore, Mel Sheridan, David Moore and Fliss Johnston.

Huge and special thanks also to a whole crew of fantastic family, friends and writing supporters, namely Eoin Devereux, Julie Hamilton, Sarah MacCurtain, James Martyn Joyce, Fergal Molony, David Moore, Paul Moore, Morgan Moore, Meredith Moore, Joe O'Connor, Clare O'Dea, Jennifer O'Dea, Joe O'Dea, Fionnuala Price, Adele Whelan and Bob Whelan.

A special note of love to Alma Rose, the newest member of our clan.

I am deeply grateful for the support of Valerie Bistany and all at the Irish Writers' Centre. The enormous privilege of the Jack Harte Bursary award has given me the gift of time and space to write at the enchanted Tyrone Guthrie Centre.

Love and thanks to my fabulous children Eoghan, Stephanie and Gabriela, and as ever, to Ger Fitz, the love of my life.

Sarah Moore Fitzgerald
January 2016